# STRANGE HOTEL

# STRANGE HOTEL

EIMEAR McBRIDE

FARRAR, STRAUS AND GIROUX   NEW YORK

Farrar, Straus and Giroux
120 Broadway, New York 10271

Printed in the United States of America
Originally published in 2020 by Faber & Faber Limited, Great Britain
Published in the United States by Farrar, Straus and Giroux
First American edition, 2020

Library of Congress Cataloging-in-Publication Data
Names: McBride, Eimear, author.
Title: Strange hotel / Eimear McBride.
Description: First American edition. I New York : Farrar, Straus
    and Giroux, 2020.
Identifiers: LCCN 2019055658 I ISBN 9780374270629 (hardcover)
Classification: LCC PR6113.C337 S77 2020 I DDC 823/.92—dc23
LC record available at https://lccn.loc.gov/2019055658

Our books may be purchased in bulk for promotional, educational, or
business use. Please contact your local bookseller or the Macmillan
Corporate and Premium Sales Department at 1-800-221-7945, extension
5442, or by e-mail at MacmillanSpecialMarkets@macmillan.com.

www.fsgbooks.com
www.twitter.com/fsgbooks • www.facebook.com/fsgbooks

10   9   8   7   6   5   4   3   2   1

*For William*

# STRANGE HOTEL

*London?*

*Paris* x

*St Petersburg*

*Moscow*

*Budapest* x

*Bratislava* x

*Warsaw* x

*Cracow* x

*Haworth* x

*St Austell* x

*Beijing* x

*Tokyo* x

*St Petersburg* x

*Bucharest* x

*Craiova*

*Paris* x

*Khartoum*

*Barcelona* x

*Cairo* x

*Riga* x

*Amsterdam* x

*Milan*

*Florence* x

*Sorrento* x

*Naples* x

*Rome* x

*Avignon* x

*Santarcangelo di Romagna*

*Brussels* x

*Siena* x

*Bagno Vignoni*

*Venice*

*Berlin* x

*Dublin*

*Donegal*

*Ballycastle*

*Belfast*

*New York* x

She has no interest whatsoever in France. The subject is unbroachable with her. She disregarded it as best she could on the train from Nice. She did not absorb her cab ride here. With this indifference, of course, she has defeated herself: tomorrow will mean the acquisition of a map. The, as yet, avoidable worse though would be requesting directions in her tense-less French. It galls – the merest suggestion of this and the insufferable tone it habitually elicits. With a shudder, she calls to mind a previous incident of 'Madame, shall we start again . . . perhaps in English this time?' Too late, too late will be the cry. But as she inwardly simmers her fractious eye alights on a bowl of matchbooks nearby – crimson, gold and gratis, liveried for the hotel. Their reverse addressed, surely? Location marked on a street grid? Retrieving two and flipping one she discovers it is. So,

5

upon sliding them between the folds of her valise, finds a complication resolved.

This appeasement aside, the foyer sags with humidity unleavened by the indoor trees. Palms, she supposes. Fronds dust-patinaed to rust, as though some off-Riviera *Death in Venice* were the desired effect. Should this be the case they've not been entirely unsuccessful, she reflects – the aqueous decadence of old Venice excepted, alongside any perceptible increase in the likelihood of an untimely death. Th. And there it is, death again. Displaying its feathers as the always inevitable. Even here, in this suppurating suburban hotel to where she herself doesn't know how to get. Enough however, enough of that. This kind of thing could make her blink but before it can she recalls her previous assessment that, however stifling the atmosphere may be, it's unlikely to bring about her demise. Besides which, there appears to be a dearth of golden-haired boys upon whom to unhealthily dwell. In fact, as she casts about, she sees absolutely no children at all. Naturally she finds in this no cause for complaint having, in her own small way, contributed to their absenteeism too. To be perfectly frank – as she is to herself – the, approaching fetid, adult clientele also fail to seriously assert their presence, beyond peripherally. An unwelcome thought this, the thought of them: walking, being, unconsciously imbibing the air as though it's a rightful allocation of theirs which will never run down. But then, above, a fan kicks in. Its whirr invasive. Air imitates motion. Time reasserts itself. Sweat rolls down her neck. It brings to mind her much favoured attitude of haste – not that she's in any specific rush. It's merely her preference not to indulge mortality's by now routine assaults on her carefully habituated ennui – a good word, ennui, so one–nil to French. This timely revival indicating, however, that now it's best the brass call bell gets repeatedly pressed and the concierge is delivered a long look of impatience. As he indicates the desk clerk's imminent attendance, she drums her fingernails almost to dents on the dark, high polished wood. Having come so far, with so little delight, she embraces this brief performance of her magnified distaste for delay.

The clerk arrives, sunned-brown and neat and slow, through the door behind the desk. His disinterest does not regard her particularly while, invested in her own, she does not regard him back. Framed in keys, who is he to me, this arbiter of rooms? Besides, she's already booked hers with some specificity and therefore need not gaze up hopefully for favour in his eyes. Well fortified thus, she slides her passport across. Her credit card after that. And as soon as the tan hand languidly indicates, swiftly signs without flourish along the dotted line. Neat fingers pass keys and hers, pale, intercept. She

7

does not look into them for the number, just goes where his point – the white tips elegantly signalling stage right. She already knows where. This is not her first time in this hotel but she had not expected to return.

The ground-floor corridor. Its hot dun gloom. The carpet runner and rods beneath her feet.

Against all inclination, she remembers its brown tinted glass, the outsize faux Ming vases in gilt willow pattern. She seems to recollect how the nylon awnings stretched to construct channels of respite from the sun. She possesses little interest in the doings of the sun – bodies spit-stretched beneath, skin crimpling to burnt umber from – but recalls how her silently professed repugnance had borne little weight on the matter before. Rather, a radiant torture appears to remain the hotel's aim, prosecuted most effectively by a marked absence of even the most cursory blind. She remembers that. Thinking that. So now does she think it afresh? And can she think it afresh? Or only ever again? Rat running around its run over and over and Stop. An instant of regret, forced from the knowledge that allowing memory, or any of its variables, admittance is invariably a mistake. Nonetheless, and even knowing that much, time makes a ladder of her anyway. Down. The room key – not being the more modern card but cut – and how on that previous occasion she'd also

8

thought 'When was the last time you saw one of those?'
What about that cigarette burn, to the far left, was that
there? Located, unusually, in the skirting board. Surely
she would remember a peculiarity like that? Does she
remember? And if, in that past, she turns her head
away, to the right, what other oddities might she see?
Or what welcome familiarity might there be? Impatient
now though with her brain's apparent receptivity, she
encourages her irritation to grow. Familiarity is not the
ambition. Never at all, of late. In fact, she'd say she has
been at pains to let nothing embed. Surely, it's merely
human nature, travel, stress, which beckons the mind
back to that other visit? She could admit she came here
on purpose but that would mean owning to a degree of
conscious volition which she remains at pains to deny.
And. On that first visit, she reminds herself, her attention had been on everywhere and so nowhere near the
now all-important imperative to forget. She just saw all
she saw and it went in and there's nothing to be done
about that.

Door. Scratched dull lock. Put in. Turn the key. Fail.
Joggle. Lean into. Be firm. Try again now. Try again,
again. And, on another try, there. She's in.

She shuts it hard behind. Abominable heat. The
day aches around her shoulders in search of other mis-
chief. Headache. Perhaps but will not do and, before

it attempts to beat this path through her, she turns the anxious air conditioning on. Once foxed by dials not of her immediate ken, she is now au fait with all the buttons of hotels and more than adept at deciphering their idiosyncrasised versions of 'Up', 'Down', 'Whirl-around', 'Press'. This time she presses. A briefly baited wait. Hum. Cool air sputters live from the vent. *In hoc signo vinces!* Well, no. Or not exactly . . . some.

In the corner, inevitably, a strapped fold-out stand for a case. Hers fits snug into the cradle. Zip. She checks for washbag damage – out of habit nowadays, rather than deep concern, and about convenience because if she had to, she could easily replace everything. Times have changed, she notes, as is her wont on these occasions of which, of late, there have been more than a few. Another unzipped bag, in another uninteresting hotel room, upon which she stares indifferently down at the folded clothes, or the shampoo congealing into them if she's been unlucky which, on this occasion, she has not. All's well in there so that's all she does, apart from extract-ing then balancing her toothpaste-spattered washbag on the too-short shelf above the low, piss-stinking loo. Scrubbed though she's sure and certainly looks it but a high turnover of dehydrated urine has a tendency to out. The poor aim of men, drunks and cracked tiles is her theory. The pungent condensation, her proof. A tightly shut bathroom door should work wonders, she thinks, and it could be so much worse. That said, she is grateful to have not yet removed her boots. Soon though she will, everything's starting to hurt. Perhaps a quick check for which make-up's gone astray first? She pulls the shaving light on. The cheap yellow fog shows her sickly but she already knew it would. Make-up's fine, almost off. There is nothing needs tending, except a quick under-eye wipe. Should she shower? She quite probably should. Not now though. She's going nowhere. She is certain of that. She turns the shave light off. Nothing to see here. She prefers it in the dark anyway.

To do. To do. She seeks tasks to do but can't find them anywhere. Look.

No need to hang up her clothes. She won't be here long enough for that. Instead the wants of sweat and thirst propagate in her head. She recalls the mini-bar not being in the obvious place but has, nevertheless, located its whereabouts after a swift moment or two. In its sole 7Up, she recognises an opportunity for restraint which she has promised herself to avail of, should the opportunity present. But, she explains to no one, it's been a very long day. Then she remembers that this has indeed been the case and grows irritable with herself for allowing no one a say. The perennial problem recurs. If only no one could be banished as easily as bade. It gets wearing, the contortions of the critic in her head to whose scrutiny she must, however, submit. She should just make the choice, as it was once previously made. She knows that. She makes it then. Sees the phone and calls to the front desk and, in overly imperative English, requests a bottle of white wine. Or two. On hanging up, she mouths, 'It's unendurable, this heat,' which her hands pretend is the directive to unlock and un-slide the fly-blown inner door. No one heard her though and did not in any regard buy this excuse.

Courtyard.

It's not a courtyard, she thinks. A wall of breeze blocks enclosing a 'bird of paradise' run amok. However, they certainly fulfil their stated remit of keeping the breeze well and truly out. And, paradisiacal as the truncated vista purports to be, she'd far rather find herself in receipt of the occasional light lickings of . . . is it the Mistral here? She can imagine that sensation described as 'delicious' by some. Never by her. It's an appropriation she finds particularly grim, as though even the pleasure of the fat is being re-consecrated by the messianic thin. At any rate, this ill-conceived digression fails to divert her for long and the lighting of a cigarette soon rekindles her preference for the feel of moving air. She suspected it would because it usually does. And she is tired. Exhausted. France appears to be taking its toll. Or her body disapproves the incidental disinterment of long, long ago. No. Just a few years ago. She wishes it was long ago though.

So instead, she makes herself of now and forswears what has been.

Meaning, here she sits, feet slipped into the grey sand beneath and already countless fag ends there. Even in their advanced state of decay she can confidently differentiate the dogged constancy of English tips from their more pliant European relatives. And, if she looks carefully does she spy a lung-collapsing papirosa there? Maybe. No matter. No matter to that, or the curl of smoke undulating over her head, all the way back in. It can linger by the ceiling. Nothing is at stake. This is France, as she's chosen. There need be no excuses made. Besides which, no other person will be in this room tonight. That is the plan. That is the plan.

Knock.

Wine knock. She knows the sound. Tentative yet authoritative. She drops and grinds the cigarette out, ensuring no spark survives. She remembers, although now does not care to remember, ensuring this too in other times. Best practice, nothing more, she counsels herself and now all gone under the dirt anyway. She gets up, straightens and goes to get. But when did the sun fall and the night rise in such hot black? Of course, she reminds herself not to be shocked, that happens so much more quickly over here.

Parquet. Pace. Light switch on and handle down.

She opens the door. Supplicatory waiter. She signs his slip. He shows the bottles to her. They're the right cold and wet after their journey from the bar. She takes them both then and does not tip. She has no euros yet. Once she would have cursed herself for this. Now, she doesn't care. The night roasts behind her and the chug in of warm air undoes the whirred cool from above.

Light switched off again.

And to the business. The accoutrements there. The corkscrew. An old one. Dig. Screw. Pull. Use pressure from the underarm and hope for the best. If it is the best, which it is, then that makes it one–all between France and her.

The bed stays unrumpled beneath as she yanks it free. A few light runnels on the bedspread. Chintz-ish brown fleur-de-lis, or cheap needlework, perhaps? There's not much she knows about that, pours, and does not spill a drop. Drink. She drinks it down with some considerable relief at outmanoeuvring her travel fatigue, the buzzing, the desiccating heat and its risk of a maudlin dusk. That's it right now, agitating her veins. Coursing through until the arches of her feet unclench – the most secret pleasure of drinking, she thinks, and unquantifiably nice. Her wrists will follow soon. Inevitably, knees. Loosed shoulders are desirable, if difficult to achieve. The key is to stop before it gets behind the eyes, after which all circumspection generally flies. That's tightrope drinking. Tonight, she will make the attempt – to unhitch from while remaining in possession of. This is her intention. Certainly, more is not in the plan and, unwilling as she is to expand on that, she has little difficulty in recollecting why. So, she will drink only until her musculature relents which, even from this starting point, will require some intransigence. She has the time for it though, probably plenty too.

Clock. She remembers over there.

Time flashes below the TV, one hour ahead. She should change her watch but why make the effort? It passes quickly enough as it is. She drifts towards what she has left behind. Who. Then decides she'd rather not. Instead she shifts her attention to the television screen and to herself within its frame. What she might resemble, lounging here, she already knows. Probably enough has become of her though for that not to count very much. And it only might be true. And equally, might not be. By now sufficient wine has been drunk to ignore no one worrying at her ear anymore. To be alone in the head is bliss. Now is the hour to take full advantage of the quiet. She lies back against the headboard and lets her legs stretch, pondering her body like an inexorable event. Until the thought surfaces that this might also not be. She takes another sip before conceding it really isn't actually and that was a foolish thing to think. Still. The body, always. She suspects she'll always in some way favour it and so, for this short while, elects to mute the perpetual fear of just how precariously life hangs by its thread. And she slips it soon enough. And finds herself quickly nudging into the next. And this she doesn't mind at all – meditating on how a few drinks bring the further joy of shearing away the female body's perpetual role as ill-fitting attire. Look in the screen at these legs, arms, even these breasts, even this stomach will do. And she is fond of her skin, although somewhat more when out of it than when firmly within. This is the way of the world, she thinks, or how the world has been, more often than she'd choose.

Never mind.

She could live days like this, in the calm relax, but when the other pang triggers, she is not surprised. She is well acquainted with the peccadilloes to which her solitude, when bibulous, inclines. This is why she's already clocked that the hotel bar is a mere two minutes' walk – right, back up the corridor. And why she knows, should it not suffice, the wider locality is likely stocked, with everything, or one, she might require. She permits this a longer than fleeting thought before the boundaries of the plan are reasserted and she opts for the breeze blocks again.

Outside, the conjugal dark romances around. Music from the bar. Bats against the moon. The wall breaks at the left, which she hadn't previously seen. There is light from the 'courtyard' next door. Fewer birds of paradise. A table and two chairs. The ribboning profile of a young man – maybe young? – with curly hair. She thinks he is smoking a Gitanes. She thinks he is looking at her. So, summoning up all her available ambivalence, she leans back against the door frame.

Warmed PVC on her spine. Smoke exhaled through her nose. Cicada click somewhere. Nip gnats or mosquitos. She is far from home or however that place may be best called to mind. Where the stuff is. Not the heart is. No, some heart is there and nowhere near enough wine has passed through her yet to make that any less true. Perhaps she does not wish it true. Or maybe just not for a while. Either way, she is untied enough to meet his eyes, briefly, then look away to the sanctuary of the distant night sky. Closing in nonetheless, too.

And thrum beyond the walls. Traffic to the east, audible but not uncomforting in its part as the perpetual route to away. For her escape is not the immediate game, content as she is to watch him shift his weight casually from the right foot to left. It appears they've simulta-neously elected not to speak. Already too late, she knows, for an 'Evening' or 'Salut', or comradely remarks about their ugly hotel and complaints about the heat. And if his eyes invite acknowledgement, there's nothing to be done about that. All she offers is a pass of glances for the span of their cigarettes. Hers ambiguous, she ensures. His, it appears, calculating the odds but, when he raises a hand, she nods. There's no further encouragement she's willing to give but . . . she is still there. And when he lights another cigarette, she lights another too. When he moves closer to the gap, she does not move. She is sure now she has ten years on him, which – at her age – amounts to nothing. Accounts for nothing too. Trawling for youth has never been her thing. In fact, her purview has been the opposite, really. But as he takes another step, looking likely to speak, she scrapes the one-third-smoked cigarette out and goes back in. As is the plan. As is that plan.

Inside, she closes the screen and assumes this does not seem dramatic or unreasonable. Who wouldn't close their screen on the multiplicity of biting things out there? And most especially because she's about to put on her bedside lamp.

But now she'd like to be busy in her body so has another drink. She'd like to reaffirm the plan so goes to the sink in the bathroom through the high-smelling air and rubs the remnants of make-up from her face. She thinks of the whiteness beneath as an absence of face. She knows this isn't true, of course, and excoriates herself for such drab submission to the inglorious work of the world. But when it suits her, it suits her to use it too. Besides, she feels that war can never be won. No. She doesn't feel that at all and that feelings are just fish to be fried. Rather she thinks, to keep herself in, she will decide to think: I could not turn myself on anyone looking like this. Again, she knows that's a lie – in the gripping moment no one's primary concern is eyeliner. So, resorting to an illogic that makes reasoned argument mute, she now says to herself: I haven't gone bare-eyed for years. But what about the life before those years? Well, that was some time ago.

Further, push further. What's as effective as self-disdain? Make-up first, now the strappings. Whittle those illusions away.

Time to take her bra off and fake relief from its dig – although the bands of red, where flesh fights the expectation of it, are surely real enough. She will not say she's no model, despite the plan, and bridles at the assumption she should honestly find this a cause for regret. If asked, she would say she is a person, a woman, and this body is the only one she's got. Thirty-five years of using and inhabiting it. Still going strong despite the life she's lived and sadly, and regretfully, she's known more than one who cannot say as much. She experiences no sense of triumph in this – possessing enough longevity to have made it into mid-life. She just thinks: leave me alone. She goes, instead, to the bedside table. She kills the bottle of wine. She puts a reasonably clean T-shirt on. She considers going outside again. Then hears several voices somewhere in the corridor beyond. It's an echo box clearly, so if they're going-to or coming-from, she cannot really tell. Conspiratorial, she thinks, happy-sounding? Her inadequate French means she cannot be sure. It forms a suspension though, makes her swallow slow. When she was young, she was mad for a group too, down the pub, summer Fridays, tapering off to chips. Her place on the periphery was rarely in doubt but she loved it all the same. The jokes of others. The stories made in her head about what transformations occurred simply by being present. What future awaited and what sophistications would grow out of herself once that future had come. She'd expected it to be opened and entered – like it would all be as simple as that. She is not sorry though, or thinks her innocence a fool, or forgets how innocence can create its own type of cruel or forgets that knowing and innocence can rub along quite happily for a while side by side. She decides to smile at this because she knows innocence never does win. Besides which, the past cannot be unpicked even if she possessed any eagerness for it and she really does not. She has almost always been a woman kneeling at the altar of 'And then?' 'And next?' A shuffle in the corridor a few doors down now. Theirs. So, they were going in. However many. For whatever reason. Some music starts up. Well, the bass anyway. Unusually she doesn't become irate at the invasion of her inner ear. Sentiment must be at work somewhere, unfortunately. The seep of alcohol and sense migrates to the days and life after life in the group finished, the life of moving on to only one. The one and only, as she'd thought of him. Don't. Don't think of that. Too late. She already has. And remembered how she'd welcomed it, the construction of complex circles of her own. Their. Their circles. Spun and spun. She'd banked on them lasting a lifetime but they had managed only some. They'd managed enough though that she's unlikely to forget and has not. It's the reason she regulates her orbit at an angle to all that. Pleasanter on the eyes, and life. Christ! These walls must be paper thin. Come on. In the morning she thinks she'll probably eat a few croissants. Come on. Will she have jam? Yes, that's right. She might well have them with jam, if they have it . . . will they? She'll have to wait, with bated breath, to see. Right now, she decides on more wine.

Now there's a snap in her celery, a spring in her step. She's passed through the mawkishness to where the sugar is going great guns in her blood. She does not think she can get very drunk. A plateau has somehow been reached. Yet, she drinks some water, to pace herself. A nod to the plan she is still in possession of. One more cigarette then she'll head for bed and everything's worked out fine! She knew it would. A little self-restraint but not punitive amounts. And this cork slides out so easily now. It could almost be a sign. She doesn't believe in signs. She pours very carefully, to proclaim her sobriety intact. The result is the very same.

Out.

Outside the sky's a horror of fight and bruise. Velour black, pumped with racket, gored by orange. She lets the heat, though, tempt her in. Less blast oven to it now and more ember, although questions about what's burnt there remain. No. Do not remain. Have been dealt with by the plan. A plan without a B. Simple to follow. In each circumstance recollectable. As she does even now, and despite the sound of the gritty slide open of next door. These doors could fall forward, it feels like. Or like they may already have done and been slotted back in until the next fall-out. Engineering has never been a preoccupation but they do seem to wobble and hotels . . . you know . . . However, with nothing to be done about that, she lights her cigarette up and, escaping the tedium of contemplation, settles into the centre of the world.

Hello.

Good evening.

How are you?

I'm fine.

She knows that his glance and her body combine. She has been here before so there's no meeting of minds she would less willingly pretend to pursue. Indifferent to this, he lights up too, as she knew he would, ushering in the beginnings of dance and excuse. Both expected and clung onto until the very last. She knows how quickly the time can pass between too soon and too late. She has the plan but appreciates he knows nothing of that. 'And you?' She can't help it or liking the dance. It's the lift she can't resist, secure in the knowledge the plan sits in place to avoid any trouble produced. So, she looks through the gap right into his face. Smiles into the smile she knows awaits. There, seen. And seen. Bodies usually go to where this look leads but she takes all the time of it she wants. She can tell he's practically there, doing the maths of her and where. His other smile. His body shifts. He pretends to be searching out his English. She guesses he doesn't have to look hard. It's just a few seconds in which to hide stepping forward. That's a honed skill but no less enjoyable for it. There's pleasure in knowing she's read it right – she could, and she sees that. A lick of hormone. She'd like to. She's fairly certain she'd enjoy it too, until no one wakes in her ear. How has she gotten this close? Why did she come out here? It just could be nice – nothing hefty, without risk and so hived off from everything else as to almost not exist at all. No one doesn't buy this excuse. No one knows her too well and that she doesn't give a toss for nice, not really, because no one's head is screwed on. 'May I join you?' rings through the gap. No one follows her eyes, then reminds her sharply: What you did once, in this room – or one so like it as to be virtually the same – this would not be that. And that . . . is not the plan. That, in fact, is the why of the plan and you shouldn't have to be told.

So, no, to him.

Yes, to herself – if this were an advert for some kind of self-help.

Bloody no one. Is there no escape?

Actually, I was just going in but . . . have a nice evening.

What a pity but . . . you too.

This, despite the expectancy in how he still waits. She finishes up her cigarette, snuffs it out in the grey sand beneath, curatorially nods her goodnight, then rises and steps back indoors. No one, it seems, is capable – and from wherever she stands – of getting anyone ignored. Further to this, no one ensures, once she's inside, that she lets the inner door slide. Shut. Tight. That she locks it loudly. That she makes of it a point of pride to do this without apology. Because, no one reminds her, she isn't sorry, not really. She has nothing to apologise for. But, just beyond no one's reach, she thinks . . . well . . .

No.

The stink of bathroom floor. The smallness of her case. All the hours of getting here and . . . and . . .

. . . now the room seems even browner than before. That's the difficulty; plans sabotage odd stealths of enjoyment, inevitably. No matter. No matter. She says it again. She retains her privacy, self-possession, and a nearly full bottle of wine. Fill the space. Flood the mind. She'd like a radio, or music, anything to barrow the assembling muddle from her head. No such option appears to exist. So, dusty barefooted, she permits herself to rumple the sheets, fill her glass to the brim and lay her head on the beige patterned pillow, down. From dimensions beyond the breeze blocks, lights throw shadows above. A paradise of birds? Of bars? She's too tired to decipher of what. Her tongue cleaves a swallow of wine to her palate, then lets it trickle down too. In a while it will become her. She's now patiently awaiting that time.

And it comes. Into itself. As it always will. Her eyes inch back to the glass and, suddenly, she is . . .

Roll. There is no one to see you roll and roll right off the bed. As your arches roll across the mock parquet. As your knees do not exist. As your shoulders open like you have wings. As your brain starts to lead from the back. As your body notices space is a trick. As your fingers wrap around the remote. Turn it on. TV. Zapped into light. Whither now? Abroad, to French television tonight. The dark. And hotel rooms alone. Everyone knows what that means.

Primarily pinkly personnelled pornography. Popularly, perseveringly and – periodically perceivably painfully – protractedly pursuing previously private perspectives of perfectly pumped penii practically pummelling professionally pruned pudenda and precisely depilated, pucely pert or – more pedantically – patently pedestrian posteriors alike. Period – as in Full Stop, and not of the bleeding kind.

You are not American, and this is stupid.

But.

Principles carry no precedence here.

But.

Phraseology is not the priority.

But.

Punctuation is in no way the point.

But.

But what?

I like what I see.

And as it goes into her, ideas resurrect of next door. Other outcomes could still be available to her. She knows, were she yet keen to try, it wouldn't be too late to change her mind. She probably won't though. She'll be better off sticking to whatever her addle recalls of the rapidly fragmenting plan. Certainly, she retains wit enough to recognise the better of bad worlds is this. And actually – now no one's done chewing her ear – does the impetus exist any longer? Hard to know. Almost nothing does. Behind, behind the eyes. Too late now, too late will be the cry. Alas, the moment has arrived to succumb to her descent. She'd badly rather call it her descant but, even in this state, she remembers she cannot sing.

Slip then.

Slip right down.

Then she feels it in the parts of herself where feeling still exists. And she likes the sensation, plus the simple filth, unhinderedly being at one with it. Unbolted in her body and seceding from thought. Patterns hint that by morning her position may have altered but tonight, she can live like this. Will. So, my hand does the strange familiar until my eyes have grown tired of the screen.

The encroach of boredom never takes long but its accelerant, the participatory loss of the mind, remains the best absence of all. Even buckling forward into its end, I do not spill my wine. Have. Have it. Lose it a little. Lose it entirely. Gone. A moment. A moment. Now, quickly sequester my sprawl. Limbs. Knickers. Put the glass safely down. Set a match to inklings of thinking about . . . but then go to sleep. And not the sleep of the just. Nor the sleep of dreams. Where the brain lies undiscerning of everything, is that even sleep?

Sound.

Down.

Down.

Down.

Sleep.

Something.

Sound.

Noise.

Clamour.

Cacophony.

And so pervasive now, she opens her unwilling eyes. Is it inside her? No, outside her. It's not of the mind. Then where? Outdoors? No, indoors. The sun is so bright. How come she's so parched? Brown blinds up. Curtains wide. Yesterday's T-shirt somehow grown tight. Sex audible everywhere.

Oh.

Eyes look. No. She can't turn her head. Fingers look and, efficiently, find the remote. Down by her side. There on the bed. How does it work? Luckily there is an instinct and it navigates swiftly to OFF. The welcome silence also comes as a shock, as the escalating moans are arbitrarily shut up, forever unconsummated now. But that's their own problem. It's her ears' reprieve – the cooling quiet in which she begins collecting herself. She's here on her own, which makes the plan a success. By the sound of it, next door is now boiling his kettle. For tea or coffee? her re-forming brain idles. Tea or coffee? Oh.

She can hear his kettle boil, then pins dropping all over France.

Oh God oh God. Why is the night? The body yes but not much else left intact. Was that the plan? Why would that be the plan? Why would she ever make a plan like that?

She knows from precedent what comes next so sits up, electing to listen to life next door instead. And hears it. Clearly. He's already up and apace. His shower-curtain rings clatter, clearly, open and shut. So clearly, in fact, she's certain she could identify exactly which type they are. She doesn't hear him sing in there but if he did, she would. Clearly. She hears the water flow, stop. She

29

hears him step out and the towel snapped from the rail. Clearly. She imagines his waist. She can't actually hear any coffee getting made – spoons, stirring – but, because of the kettle, thinks he probably does. What she next clearly hears is the metal strap of his watch, picked from the desk? Maybe? The side table perhaps? Hears it wrung round his wrist until its clasp clicks. Clearly. So clearly, she hears this, that the only room left within her for self-deceit now collapses completely in. There is no possibility, she admits, of her 'entertainments' having gone unheard, unless . . . Unless? Why bother herself? Too late, too late is already the cry. Ear plugs or earphones or Valium or what? Dance and excuse. Why did she choose the latter last night? The hard end, the steep side, the long way round. How do so many others never get this wrong? Why do so many others see these problems a mile off and so go a mile out of their way? She is tired. No. Avoiding the truth. No. She's just been here before. In this place, which she's now ruined. Only once. Not in ages. Not in years. It amounts almost to nothing, those twelve, thirteen hours but. But. But. But. They never will return again. And from here she can see right back to here, but then. To the way he swore at the tyre. To the grease under his nails. How they had found it in the middle of some very weird rain. 'Birds of paradise?' he'd suggested when she'd racked for the plant's name. 'This place is so grim,' he'd said, after he'd ordered some wine, and she'd said, 'It'll be fine.' 'Oh yeah,' he'd said, 'it'll be fine.' Which, in fact, it was. All of it was. And far more than that.

Next door zips his case up and she is recalled. To head hanging, hand wringing, the whole medley of awful. It's too soon to reframe last night as a blank but she'll try to just as soon as she can. Because that is the plan. That is now the plan. But in the mode of confession, and given all that has passed, can she truly say coming round on his side of the wall would have been so much worse? If she's being honest, and she thinks she is. Maybe though she's not ready to think. Just leave it for now, knowing there'll be an assessment, in due course, some other time. In this moment there is only spectacular shame. Blah blah. I've come to talk to you again. Etc. Etc. Ad infinitum, and beyond. France has won the match.

She hears his door open, then close. Turn of a key, old-fashioned key, in its lock. She follows the tread of his footfalls right up the corridor, with its strange frame of light and its microphone logic, until expensive shoes strike the tiles of the foyer floor. Then stop. At the desk? His just about audible salutation receives a conspiratorial 'Salut'. She recognises the clerk's voice and hears knowing in it. He knows. He heard. Everyone did.

Then even her poor French makes out a question about breakfast. Where they serve it, she thinks and Oh God.

Oh God. Breakfast.

Has she paid for that, or not? Inevitably she's suddenly empty. She is completely starving. She won't leave this room though. She absolutely cannot. The merest glance across the breakfast room would eviscerate her now. But can she bear to call for room service? Or is that just, not yet? She checks her watch. She checks herself. She thinks there's still time to decide.

*Orford* x

*Manchester* x

*Edinburgh* x

*Dublin*

*Dingle*

*Liverpool* x

*Bristol*

*Dublin*

*Galway*

*Sydney* x

*Listowel*

*Borris*

*Cork*

*Dublin*

*Galway*

*Prague*

There are more cobbles down there than you could ever wish for, she thinks, no wonder defenestration was a thing. She has no doubt, if each could speak, their mouths would yawn fantastic with history. But, in truth, hers is a beggared interest. Missives from antiquity are not why she's here and, if more rigorous motives yet remain unclear, she is at peace with that. She can be, and can choose to be, in any given place. Furthermore, she's a grown woman and no body exists to which she must report back on every instant. Too much already of that though. Far too much, she thinks, her scorn rising at the redundant aegis of her instincts. All she really wants is the dark behind her eyes and perhaps for the rain to relent.

Unfortunately, with neither appearing imminent, in the short term she must take solace in her cigarette. In with pleasure, out with smoke – if not exactly how the saying goes, illustrative, certainly. In the medium term she may contemplate those cobblestones unfurling across the ways and alleys for as far as she can see. And, from the well-placed height she is, she can see quite far. She plans to remain in the short and medium term as long as she can because if there is a longer term it would be news to her. That said, she'd welcome any indication of its presence, intimating – as it surely would – some part of her knows something of what she does. But unedified by this insight, she attempts to shake it off – while still maintaining some appreciation that it is most likely true.

True too however, and equally so, is that the tiny balcony she finds herself outside on now is almost open to the elements. She hadn't bargained on that before stepping out. Glass panels, she'd assumed, secured all within from without. They form window walls on either side, pressed into the concrete and, to be sure, ivied but seemingly sturdy enough. Only a lip at the front edge though where panes must have been. Where have they disappeared off to then? Might they have fallen out, causing chaos on the streets and making the city dream again of Hussites or Catholics? More prosaically, they've probably been taken in for repair. Negligent, she thinks, allowing guests access out here when, between the inner sliding door and eternity, there's little more than a thin brass rail. Had she known this was the state of play, she'd have certainly stayed in. Careless of her not to check, especially with the heavens already disgorging themselves all over everywhere. On reflection, that solitary, canker-black ficus should have given her pause.

But then who in this climate tries to grow one of those outdoors? Realistically, if she'd noticed, she'd probably have blamed the fag ends in its pot. The verdigrised rail should have also prompted some thoughts but . . . No matter now, any of this, as her bare back shivers in the starched solid sheet which her fingers entangle as rope. She should really go in and get a few clothes on or, at least, step back from the looming inundation pattering down, a hair's breadth from her nose. That is all quite right and she should do that. Take either option, or both, if she feels like it.

She hesitates instead.

She would rather be by herself and inside there's still render in the air so it won't feel like it yet. And also, she's not. Although, maybe she is? Perhaps he's gone? She doesn't really think he has and knows even pretending it casts an unflattering light on her ability to assess. Only the most delusional hope imagines it could go either way. Still, pursuing it she recreates the sound of him coming out of her bathroom and then of her door clicking closed somewhere behind. Realistically of course, this could be sourced from anywhere, any time. She possesses no ear for the variation of such mechanisms, of either the domestic or international kind. This becomes doubly vexatious once she factors in Time – which she always must because it keeps her at its whim whenever she is not taking charge. So, click! She hears it. But now or then? Far back or of late? Real? Or a manifestation of some demeaning need, transposing itself, having a laugh at her expense? She knows Time delights in wasting her portion of it, but also that she doesn't have to concede. This is a lesson she has already learned, well.

Well, well.

But how to get from here to making it happen, getting him gone?

Might it help to simply put her foot down?

It might, but she suspects it won't.

In her role of the least resistant, she has made herself strong. There can be scenes after all, or there can just be done. She has developed a marked preference for that. Also, logic decrees that whichever way she might act he can't be too much longer now – and where there's already awkwardness aplenty there's never any call to prolong the agony. But, in case he proves sluggish she'll linger here, killing time with the lie that it's not to avoid him, it's simply to double-check. As she has just said, there's nothing to be gained by the gratuitous exacerbation of pressure. How glad she is to have also learned this lesson. For despite it being one she still on occasion forgets, she will not do so tonight. She is ahead of herself. Until she is alone, or certain she is, she will tolerate the Czech damp and listen out for his progress through the rain against the glass. Not pitter-patter now. More cats and dogs. And with a veritable howl beginning to get up, hammer and tongs before long, she expects. Most definitely audible everywhere. Most definitely audible to him.

Really?

Yes.

This hotel is old and not particularly spacious. He can certainly hear the rain.

She calmly envisages his reaction from inside that pokey bathroom. She hopes it will spur him to speedier action. How long can it take to put on pants anyway? She doesn't seem to recall anything conspicuously complex about them. Of course, at the time they hadn't exactly been the subject of her diligent examination. Why would they though or could they have been? Nonetheless, she dredges from the back of her mind . . . a button fly . . . and he did have a belt but, again, nothing complicated. So . . .

She really wishes he would hurry up.

In order to do that though, she must first admit the wishful thinking of which she has been guilty. There is absolutely no way she really heard that room door click. He is still in there, doing whatever it is he is. Therefore she, in her abject cowardice – speedily reframed as an all-absorbing female patience – is obliged to abide where she is. Waiting. Listening. She will, doubt-less, soon arrive at the self-justifying. She possesses a genuine horror of her propensity for that but, having rebuffed its earlier attack, is somewhat more confi-dent of turning its advances aside. She is pleased with this idea – and despite the reactiveness it suggests – encourages further mutations of it. Yes, perhaps she should face the situation head on? Go inside and draw his attention to the incipient torrent? Not to insist he hurry, merely to chivvy him along. Maybe suggest, if he's quick, he might still get home before the very worst of it hits? This is based on the assumption, of course, that he lives in the vicinity. It's also made without any underlying acquaintance with his situation re transport, accommodation or preferred exit etiquette. That said, isn't this generally how assumptions work? A quick extrapolation made for the purposes of suiting yourself? See? See that? She can make them too. Him not actually being here to take receipt of them though makes it an empty sort-of triumphalism for her and its sole ricochet remains in her head.

Anyway.

Whenever he goes, and wherever he may live, she truly hopes he will manage it. Getting soaked would probably prove his back-breaking straw of the night and in the street, trees are shivering now with every indication he might.

Unless, of course, he *has* actually gone.

Her heart rises again to a hope which, in a moment, her good sense will destroy. But in this brief return to the friendly shores of self-deceit, she tells herself that if she looks over the balcony, she might see him come out down there. Even taking the hotel lift's inefficiency into account, it would not be too much longer now – as long as the click she has clearly invented were real. And if he were not to stop, say, for a snack or light meal at the insalubrious restaurant below. Assuming too he is not the kind of man for whom hotel bars prove irresistibly attractive, which he may well be. She doesn't know him sufficiently to more than speculate. But as this night is generally inching her towards placing unsafe bets, she decides she will.

So, she steps a little closer to the edge and searches for his familiar figure down there. As a stranger herself she does not expect to recognise any other than his. Windows. Coving. Cobbled streets. The awning gets in the way but the lighting helps. There's not much to-ing and fro-ing either because of the deluge. So, for those inclined to look there are no real deterrents to sight. Provided he leaves via the front entrance he should be easy to spot. And why wouldn't he? It's the quickest way out.

She'd use it if she were him – that she isn't has already been established so is tiresome to reiterate. Could that be? Under the umbrella? No . . . it's not. That's some other man – probably the staunchly leaving sort. Hers wouldn't ferry about a collapsible umbrella, she hypothesises but, again, how could she possibly know? He might be extremely practical, or meticulous about his clothes or delicately constituted. On repeat now: how would she know? His body was certainly very slim. Of the wiry variety however, she'd reckoned – rather than indicative of any lack of robustness, physically. But, even if you want to know, you can't be sure – and she hadn't wanted to know – because you can't ever know what's going on inside a body, even your own. What might be holding up well or going wrong. At least until after, and then you might think, 'Actually that probably shouldn't have been quite so unforeseen.' But it's rare for people to think those things, she thinks. She definitely hadn't been thinking them about him. Plus, those kinds of thoughts have a tendency to become time-consuming especially, having always liked them tall, and tall men frequently suffering from What if she went over the railing right now, how long would it take her to fall? Would it even be high enough? Another thing about which it's quite hard to be accurate, especially when unfamiliar with the necessary statistics Stop.

But hadn't the defenestrated regents survived?

Oh yes.

Still, stop.

Really stop.

She does.

She fractures the thought.

She reverses her step forward to back.

It's an act of wanton precaution. She knows that but decides on it anyway.

Then she starts to collect her preferable thoughts and ensure the favoured part of her brain is in condition to commence their process. It seems to be. Therefore, she can begin.

Looking down is never a good idea. She knows this to be an objective fact. If there had been glass in there it would have been fine and not that she suffers from a fear of heights but . . . Nevertheless, history suggests, in the interval between those cobbles and her balcony rail, she would more than likely see some abyss, some great maw, opening up. She has before so she will, or may, and this knowledge is so old as to be entirely unnoteworthy now. It's the reason why she lately states a ground-floor room to be her preference, wherever possible. And tonight, it not being so, should have placed her on her guard. She has been imprudent and that's undeniable. Still, no harm done. Although she finds herself again in the disappointing midst of this, she need only set back the hands of her clock to a state of stringent anti-alarm.

Besides, it's no longer a matter of an impulse towards jumping. Nowadays it's much more about falling, an awareness of how falling might be. Not aided, she notes, by how this particular balcony, lacking some windows, stands wide open floor to ceiling – the laughably sur-mountable rail aside. See? The devil is in the detail and, on noticing this, she cannot help but estimate there is enough space through which a body could be easily propelled, if a body wanted to go. Naturally, her body doesn't want to do that. However, it apparently draws comfort from thinking about it. Which is a very bad habit. She thought she'd gotten rid of that ages ago. And, to bolster this notion, immediately decides that so indeed she has. This infelicitous relapse – if she will even term it as such – is of a different variety. This she would describe as if she has, inadvertently, permitted herself to think that just beyond as far as she can see, a darkness lies which is really a nothing and falling into it might become suddenly . . . viable.

Well now.

Alright then.

That's been said.

She's always been suspicious of her dramatic tenden-cies but surely this beats all.

And if, in the unlikely event, the notion of this 'darkness' is true? Although how could it be? Even with her view impaired by the now lashing rain, her eyes persist in still seeing something for 'as far as she can see' – making Prague's spires worth their weight in gold this evening. Furthermore, one may fall off an object but not off a city and . . . where is she finding all this? She should be scrubbing it off not pursuing. Not permitting it to unfold and feeding it oxygen. She knows all that but in the lower depths, she thinks, 'Really, how would it really be?' What? To fall off into nothing. To take, in full knowledge, the step. But her shallows, coming to her rescue, ride in with their traditional counterattack. They rebuke her for the melodrama she continues to generate – ridiculously. Yes, they say, 'ridiculously' is the only word. Falling off into nothing? Whoever has cause to ask a question like that? Falling off into nothing is most probably like absolutely nothing at all. You need know no more as there's no more to know. We'll say nothing else on the matter and neither will you. Recognising a good point when she hears one, yes, she stubs out her cigarette. Ha!

And even if she did say more – which she will not – it would merely be to observe that too late, too late then would be the cry of all that excess of emotion, just as now. What's the purpose of reiterating this to herself anyhow? As though she's not already, and evidently, outlived her use for feeling. Fun while it lasts, of course, like every permutation of sex – and why must she, with such frequent vulgarity, return to that? – but ultimately an overindulgence which she has strictly forbidden herself.

Better that.

Firmer ground.

She likes herself callous.

She pulls the sheet tight, finding pleasure in the discomfort of watching her fingertips turn white. She will not keep on till they're blue. She won't choke the life from them. They are useful. However, given the word 'pleasure' was there, feeling is once again implied. Purely of the physical sort though she would claim and physical feeling is completely fine. Apparently. How come? 'That . . . that . . . that,' she says, 'is entirely different.' Physical feeling is not just in her head. Is not just a given manner of processing experience. It is life itself and without which there is none. Which is, in fact, a simplistic invention but she is beginning to think the time for this digression is up. She should really be getting off this subject. In order to, she recalls that, after previous glitches of this type, she just went forward and that was the point. Eventually. No. Willingly. She was willing to go forward. She always is. Is that so? Again, she thinks: let's change the subject. How did I ever manage to arrive at this? Dead pot plants, absent windows and rain and imagining that man going out into it and the shape of his body and the past and . . .

Well, whatever trail of breadcrumbs led up this path, it was extremely stupid and without any purpose and either way doesn't really matter now and she had just . . . better recall . . .

No.

No.

Something else.

She's better off having no truck with these inverted chats. Why does she start into them anyway? Perhaps this is the self-justifying phase and she has fallen, accidentally, in?

Very possibly.

Well then.

She had better get out.

She is at the mercy of nothing, she reminds herself. Everything, everything lies where it lay. She can probably even work up a rational explanation for that one irrational thought, or was it two? Aren't 'How long would it take her to fall?' and 'Would it even be high enough?' in fact separate? Really, they're two sides of the same question. But, best leave the pedants to argue the difference. There must be something more productive she can do? In a bid then to resurrect this to something from nil, she dredges up the wiles of vertigo. And she considers this is a completely reasonable place to go in a mind that's just given itself a fright.

But then.

Even that . . .

What?

Vertigo has its own rules for debate.

For instance: is vertigo the fear of heights or the fear of an irresistible desire to jump? Or both? Or neither? She should know. She certainly did. She explicitly remembers explaining it once to a child, for an essay, for school. So, she presumes she must have known. Perhaps she just absent-mindedly looked it up – which would explain its seeming irretrievability now. But she's fairly sure she would not have told that child an untruth. A lie of omission is possible, of course, but that would have been at the worst.

Ah.

Do this or not?

The worst may be unpalatable but must remain on the table because . . . well . . . when all's said and done . . . it may not have been the best time for thinking about them; heights or falls. Even now, so much later, she should have known to show greater circumspection near that ledge. However, if the truth is – as she's just insisted *is* the

46

case – that everything still lies where it lay, that the past is immobile and can never be resuscitated, she's at liberty to think about it as much as she likes. She doesn't imagine she will but, were she so inclined, she might admit that the thought of a jump had occurred to her most days, for maybe a year and a half – the thought that she could, or that she even might. Not to mention randomly calculating the height of whatever building caught her eye. No, not to mention that. But, actually, now that it's too late not to think about it, every day would be more accurate. And on some days, every hour. Some hours, every minute. And really, for two years or more.

But that's a long time away now. That's a very long time in the past and, being a differently constituted 'long' to, say, that of distance, it possesses no automatic right to be seen. And yes, she is aware this has become a cumbersome theme – which does not sit well with her stern rejection of self-justifying tendencies. I suppose, she thinks, sometimes you just make a mistake and sometimes this branches into branches until you're so far away that you have no idea how to get back. In this assessment she can agree with herself, apart from the part which she can't. This is the part which knows, and knew, she always had to decide what was next.

Hmmm.

Whenever she's previously had to decide between

thinking of the near or distant past, the near has generally been her first port of call. However, in this instance, it may be meet to dwell upon longer ago. Perhaps this even suggests clues being pieced together by her unconscious? She can't deny she'd be happier with an incontestable conclusion about why tonight went so rapidly downhill. These things don't tend to, usually, for her. Not anymore. And not to suggest that they are events which she meticulously orchestrates. Indeed, impulsivity is most often the guiding tool. But there is a rhythm to how these things go and tonight was not an exception – as far as she can tell. Until suddenly it was and there was no chance of a face-saving extrication for her. There was only what she said. To be fair, it was in response to what he had. She isn't embarrassed. She did not over-react. She will stand by this, which does little to unpick the mysterious, deeper discomfort she seems to be experiencing now. Really though, she's becoming impatient with how much time she is wasting on this.

She should get to bed.

She should get to sleep.

She should get in out of this cold before she catches her death.

She doesn't move.

She lights another cigarette and snatches another peer over the edge, in spite of her mock vertigo.

Down with the rain to the sloping streets and further on to down the hills. Down to a river streaked with antique bridges and on from there down to the sea – perhaps via many other countries but this pan out of the journey is essentially the same. Trickling from a source to the rolling end. To far, far out and the no going back. She sees nothing down there but the sodden night. No one she knows crosses the cobbles the puddles hide. She wonders if the rain is turning to sleet? By herself, she still modestly pulls up her sheet. A sudden new light from behind casts her shadow out. His dreamt-of departure from the bathroom perhaps coming to pass – which is welcome news – but casts her outline monstrous onto the deserted streets of Prague. Does she jump or is she pushed? Neither. She knows this, as well as not to follow such an unhelpful line of thought. She shrinks back instead and the shadow shrinks too, until she is again more woman than ghoul. It was appropriate enough for this place though, she thinks; with its defenestrations and golems and pulverised Springs. And other occurrences, other visits, by others in other times. Less momentous in the world but it is the little things which make each life up in the end.

What does she mean by that?

It's hard to explain even to the other half of her brain, which this half feels somewhat bound to fill in.

So, have a think.

Have a go at it like this:

Sometimes she forgets all the places she's been until someone asks and she'll remember then. Then remember that what she's been regarding as bedrock has, in fact, acquired sediment. No, she hadn't been there once but now she has. The time for not knowing about it has passed, and often considerably, on. She likes to think this happens only about countries, allowing her to enjoy recalling that she has indeed travelled and is no longer the girl who's never been anywhere. When this happens it's a real, and valuable, pleasure but is also not the only occasion it happens to her. She keeps so little of her past bonded close that she frequently has cause for surprise. Here lies a whole slab of your life you've completely left out in the cold. Not on purpose, out of cowardice or shame. Not, in fact, for any good reason she can name. Except there was youth and then there was later but only youth got to dig its claws in.

She's sure there are many wise explanations for this. She has been offered them and explored them and she finds them lacking, to be frank.

She's heard it's to do with 'getting older' or lines on the face, or greyer, or the hideous 'thickening around the waist'. It's about finding it harder to get pregnant – which she does not even want. It's having too many children or not enough. Being with someone too long or too long without. It's disparities in the workplace. Professional failure, or success. It is that despite every-thing, all that's been accomplished and all that's been missed and all the accretions of the life that's been lived, for a woman in her early forties, unhappiness is what's assumed to be in store. That, and the mandatory belief in a younger face behind her face which is the only place where the possibility of any happiness resides. She really admires the effort and co-ordination it surely required to make this belief as rottenly insidious as it is now. But she does not believe it and objects to the assumption she ever would.

Then she hears him move into the room behind but thinks of the rain instead.

Harder now. Pounding almost. Comfort in that, she thinks as she is often inclined. In childhood it was safety and being inside while the world went wild out there. These days it's the washing off of histories past. The feet that have walked these streets. What weights they carried and, whatever they may have been, how those lives have vanished. Some from sight. Some from mind. So many even from the genetic sludge of mankind and yet once they were as she now is. Looking where she looks. Waiting for events. And were disappointed or were impressed or just became distracted by something else and failed to see any of it at all. She could, if she wanted, imagine so much. She could remember who exactly she's thinking of, who came to this city long ago. She could put herself in his place and draw a good guess at his impressions of it back then. She could pluck them right out of thin air. She has so much information stored within her. So many apertures in memory through which to see. Uselessly now, she supposes, except for fantasies like this, which serve no good purpose beyond causing upset. Being younger would be no remedy for this. Being older might.

But who does she think she kids with this stuff? She should know better. She is old enough.

And she does.

So, she turns aside from this noxious recreating of the past. And, to cut the air supply off, refuses to specifically locate that thought in the when or who. She'll simply say instead that she could. She could conjure those things up – as anyone with imagination and willing might. However, she has neither the desire nor impetus for it. She prefers to move forward, on to the next and the next thing is: is that the wind getting up? Howling a bit, like it knows to distract? Remember how he used to stoop against it? This extra rumination she stops dead in its tracks.

Is it possible you have somehow not heard myself speak?

To be clear then, enough of this.

Uncooperative though, it continues to maraud and assert its vague right to be heard. Think of. Think of. No I will not. And, unwilling for her own brain to leave her outfoxed, she peers into the weather again. It is stormy and effectively diverting.

Then more activity-indicative sounds issue from within. The uncooperative portion of her night is surely done. She will not turn, in order to avoid further exchange but she is grateful to now be thinking about this which, although awkward in the extreme, is greatly preferable.

So then, evaluation, stake your claim.

It takes a moment to formulate its question but gets there in the end.

What is there to be learned from tonight's miscarriage of fun? Well, Doctor, it is a thorny one. She thinks she was as explicit as she could've been from the earliest on so she cannot attribute it to a lack of communication. He'd seemed bright enough not to arrive with any inexplicable assumptions and, initially, gave no indication he had. As far as she's concerned, the first stage was fine. Both bodies performed exactly as planned. In fact, in every way as well as she'd hoped. He had also seemed happy enough. It was only afterwards things took a turn for the worse. She hadn't intended to hurt his feelings. To be honest, she's not even sure if she has. Well, obvious interpretations of knitted brows and the snatching-up of discarded clothing aside, how could she be? She is also without inclination to press. She has absolutely no interest in violating what is private, his feelings are his business alone. She just wishes he hadn't presumed she possessed quite so many of her own. She has some, naturally, but spread thinly around – with few kept available for these kinds of encounters. She is even having some now. She will admit to feeling bad for implying his sole purpose was to be conducive to sleep. Of course! She understands no one likes to think themselves a sedative and she certainly hadn't found the physical exchange soporific but . . . in the shadowy longer term . . . why else did he think he was there? That this was the start of a beautiful friendship? Actually, she's annoyed he hadn't read the situation with more care. There was no need for this peculiar turn of events. She could now be in her warm bed, half fallen asleep instead of freezing outside on this balcony, smoking like a chimney, damp from the rain, looking over the edge. No.

She is not doing that again.

She is thinking about what he said.

The madness of it. I mean, who starts all that with a one-night stand – and she will not accept he hadn't grasped the nature of their exchange. Realistically how else did he think she would respond? Answer yes then spill her guts? To him? The man she was already looking forward to making himself scarce? She never would. She is not that woman. Are you mad? And even if he had been right? But how on earth could he be? An hour spent rolling in the hay hardly opens a gateway to the realms of another's soul. Yes, now that she thinks of it 'I think you'd better go. I'm pretty tired, so you can consider your job well done' really was the only option. Not her most eloquent moment but there it is. It's not like she'd been preparing for it. He said what he said. She replied as she had. He had taken it badly – the aforementioned knit brows and shirt grabbed. Exit stage left – pursued by his huff – into the bathroom. She took a moment and then came out here. Perhaps he'd thought empathy was what she was after? Or sympathy? She can't imagine anything more unappealing. Who cares if she'd cried unexpectedly? People do. It was unconnected to him and all that had taken place in that room. It was nothing. Definitely nothing to him. An inane reaction to something she had no business thinking. She wishes he'd go so she could get in the bath.

Then speak of the devil.

There it is.

Click!

The door behind.
Unmistakeably it.
Ficus, farewell!
Not a moment too soon.
And she is . . .
Alone again.
And she thinks
Thank God.

*Edinburgh* x

*Portarlington*

*Dublin*

*Aldeburgh*

*Ubud* x

*Cheltenham*

*Calgary*

*Vancouver* x

*San Francisco* x

*Seattle*

*Austin* x

*Washington DC*

*Boston*

*Toronto*

*New York*

*Sizewell*

*Swansea*

*Belfast*

*Pulford*

*Delhi*

*Jaipur*

*Agra*

*Birmingham*

*Wolverhampton*

*Amsterdam*

*Antwerp*

*Oslo* x

Is it any light or the quality of light? she thinks, as though she is alone. As though she has hours free to contemplate this: dawn shards lengthily puncturing an ill-fitting pelmet, striating almost all the way down. Birds like beams descend the velveteen fawn? She's already regretting the prose this is bringing to mind so why further delay herself over the inadvertent aesthetic when she ought to have already gone? Could she not, and with considerably more ease, ponder similar refractions to these every bit as well in her room? While it's true that in former times she would have laid a plan – a step-by-step to up and going – in those old times, she'd have needed the prompting. In these times, she does not. She has practised to perfect, or so she'd thought. Has she now somehow developed a lag in her multi-disciplinary approach? Perhaps. A little. Nothing of any great significance, she thinks. After all, her resolve to leave is genuine enough, it's merely the utter necessity which remains in doubt . . . which, perhaps, it always had? No, she does not accept that. She hooks the eye at her throat, smooths her collar flat, then makes within herself the usual argument of custom and expectation, and these remain airtight. Nevertheless, disquiet proliferates, unexpectedly. Also needlessly, she's still inclined to suspect. She's not so fool as to misinterpret her impulse to vanish as an obligation to life and limb. However anomalous this situation has become, her long-pragmatised intuition suggests nothing untoward would happen were she to remain exactly where she is. Indeed, should she prefer to, she thinks she could – and under no particular duress to even appear circumspect – take all the time she needs. Leisure is ever, and entirely, preferable to rush. But it does beg the question, of course: for what is she taking the time? Therefore, given the incontestable fact that she already is, she decides she may as well stay put and, albeit briefly, unravel it now.

So.

Theory One: she indulges in procrastination in order to take time to dress.

This is plausible, yes, except she already is. She's even had the time to assess the degree of wrinkling to her skirt. And, although not particularly agitated by such things, she's gauged the height of the run in her stocking sufficient to evade even the most inquisitive eye. There was no fast and loose of knickers strewn, brassieres strung from the lampshade or concealed within the night's miasma of 'we got naked quick'. They hadn't, so not at all. Each item was straightforwardly to hand – for instance, both of her shoes – and slipped on. Despite the dark, and lack of mirror, her hair has received a reasonably comprehensive comb. The tiny buttons on the front of her shirt are all fastened – the aforementioned, fiddly eye as well. She can see her bag lying within reach by the door. Her coat, it is to be expected, hangs somewhere in that general vicinity too. She'd forgotten her gloves back in her room which, at any rate, had proved to be the instigator of the events of the evening and are, therefore, of no concern. So, it would seem the inventory for her proposed exodus is complete. Her worldly possessions have been accounted for. Also, her appearance – as much as possible given the circumstance – and yet, despite the complete absence of any quantifiable hindrance, she is still here. Therefore, she must apparently concede she's not dawdling in order to groom or dress. This hardly comes as a shock. She knew already it was a long shot upon which she'll now have to improve.

So, if you're sitting comfortably – and why ever might that be? – she perseveres.

Theory Two: she is taking this long to leave in order to give herself time to think.

This is obviously the next place to go but, in reality, requires a clarification further: give herself the time to think about what? Whether it was light and which type woke her up? True it catches the eye, like it can in the north, but she clearly remembers waking up in the dark with no thoughts on the style of the dawn. Besides, it's only in these last few moments that the light's begun to make itself known. So, while she's quite prepared to admit its appeal and much as she could sit and admire, its lanceolar fingers only inspire trivialities she's pondered before – musings on how the winters further up must be hard. Questions about what practicalities are required to endure in such cold. Thoughts on the psychological consequences of life without sun and its looming prospect in the preceding months. And, most obviously, uninformed assumptions about the Nordic interaction with alcohol. Nothing outlandish or especially prescient then; besides, it's not even winter yet.

Perhaps, with some latitude, it might be possible to link these unlively reflections on climatic conditions to a nostalgia for the rained skies of home? No, her instinct swiftly knows, no, it's really not, no. Therefore, it does seem unlikely that these speculations on the annual Norwegian eclipse – however mundane or philosophic – could have provoked her to this idling here. Which, in turn, means it's time to go another round.

So.

Theory Three: she is idling because of what transpired in here last night.

A PhD in human interactivity isn't required to identify the nature of what passed. A far more relevant question would be, perhaps, why would she procrastinate over that? As a physical event it's hardly a rank outlier on the continuum of cause and effect. The paths of people uninterested in mess occasionally, anonymously, intersect, then frequently painlessly, re-separate with neither party suffered to lick up any scraps or tend another's wounds. She's well aware it sounds odd to phrase it like that and that alternative interpretations abound. However, she's as ambivalent about those as the activity itself, as well as popular convictions about that activity's afterlife. Her living after has always been perfectly fine. And yet she remains. She remains in this room, as though immobilised by comfort. But this is an old bed. Laziness? Unlikely, as it's now taking more effort to languish in vacillation than go. Fear? Certainly not that. A single pang originating from there she would instantly spot and know too much about to ignore. There must be another question then, even if her interrogative thoroughness has failed to establish it yet. Perhaps she has just succumbed to an exercise in pedantry and is allowing it to get in the way? Well, maybe . . . why not?

So then, in pursuit of this.

Theory Four: She somehow thinks that language will see her through.

Not actual talk so much as a good old linguistic knot. Punctuation, sentence structure, etc. Like everyone else she was reared to rely on that empire upon which the sun, supposedly, never set. Send those good constructions out to war and then, from your lovely grammatical afar, watch them mown down by the whim of the world. From afar as possible being the emphasis – keeping words as far as possible from the scent of blood and guts. Building cathedrals around them to mask it. Sometimes digging moats. Plus, there's more camaraderie in clever construction than chaos; that's a road which must be always walked alone. She learned all of those lessons, of course she did, but ultimately could not help herself. All the words filled up with blood and moved around as though entitled to motion so she gave them the freedom of her brain. And they went running in loops and running out of arrangement or simply running until their running was done. Until they were so dissipated, or so tightly wound, that they ceased to mean anything more to her. The trick was knowing when to stop. The trick was knowing how much others could take. And then she got tired of the trick. And then she saw others using sub-standard versions of it. And then she realised that didn't really count. And then she knew she'd have to find other configurations somehow. Why is the world always such work? It's harder to let the words into her body now or, maybe, out. They used to form and re-form themselves in order to dole out whatever she had in mind, whatever the meanings her body inclined to make them make. Now, they barely carry meaning beyond the literal wattle and daub. This does, occasionally, make her wistful for the savagery of before when, beholden to no one, the words did whatever they pleased. She wouldn't mind going back to that. But there is no going back and, she suspects, the price of regaining access is one she'd now be unwilling to pay. The sight, sound, taste and smell of it all grew too much. Originally, she'd thought this was just for a while but it had become, in the aftermath of turbulent times, her preferred manner in which to proceed. Thinking her way carefully around every instant. Grammatically and logically constructing it. Even now, she can hear herself doing it. Lining words up against words, then clause against clause until an agreeable distance has been reached from the initial, unmanageable impulse which first set them all in train. She's doing it now, and now, and now, and now, and it will continue, she's certain, unto the horizon and then, indeed, beyond. Frankly, she finds it exhausting, interrogating her own interrogation. But the satisfaction she derives from her own infuriation seems to have become irresistible. The useless precision of this exasperating thought inclines her to sigh out loudly, self-impatiently, but she is mindful to not. Especially as she begins to perceive light sounds of a stirring emanating from the bed. She does not turn to check, instead braces for a trespass on her silence.

Then nothing comes of it.

She knows it is a warning though. She really should pick up the pace. If there is such a thing as luck, she must be close enough now to out. So, by all means, ransack a little further in the deep but it'll probably prove expeditious to leave the linguistic thread where it hangs. It exists alright but it's been alive for nights and nights. There's no plausible reason why this morning should be the time it chooses to unhelpfully express regret. Regret though. She was coming to that. Of course, she was. Inevitably must. All tall tales of being female insist upon it. She usually refuses but, in this circumstance perhaps, she could examine herself for any suggestions of it? However unlikely, uncovering a sprinkling might shed some light but . . . hurry now. Hurry up.

So.

Theory Five: she is taking this time in order to feel – or because she feels – regret?

Displaying a natural antipathy to this proposed logic, she aligns the buttons on her cuff. Neatened to straight now, and of some silvery metal stuff for which she has no name, she notices how they might catch the light. Might make watch-face throws on a class wall to torment some poor teacher's eye. She wouldn't have but some more troublesome classmates might and she would have laughed inside – all outward signs of rebellion reserved for the aforementioned clamorous words. In here though, looking at and thinking about this, it's a further procrastination. She is aware of it. Is she even taking her departure seriously now? Or has she succumbed to some weird notion of just falling in with whatever happens next? Surely, it's too soon for that? Not unconcerned it might be though, she elects to usher a greater practicality in. So now, pose the question again. Is she taking so much time over leaving because she is experiencing regret? She despises the very idea of it. Regret, with all its soft shame. If she *is* experiencing regret however, then regret towards whom? It's not an emotion which can hang by itself, twisting alone in the head. Moreover, what is it precisely she should be experiencing all this regret for? The manner in which she disports or comports herself is pertinent to no one and, unquestionably, not anymore. This reasoning she believes to be essentially correct and views her autonomy in this matter as little cause for upset. She prefers to think of it, when she thinks of it, as something of a relief. How pleasant to be a solitary body making its own way through time. If only this were quite as true as pat. But what person is in possession of every solution they want? And does she relish the implied finality of that choice really so very much? Yes. Or no, in a way. Of course, no immediate decision need be made. Better to allow it to continue its life as a question, if not one for answering here . . . or generally.

Another full stop, yes, but at the expense of another few valuable seconds. If she didn't know better, she'd say she had done it on purpose; employed digression as an obstructive. Not an entirely unreasonable assumption as it has plainly left her still sitting in this room. None the wiser either and only more anxious that irresolution is becoming an end in itself. To avoid this disaster, she insists she pull herself together. Then wonders if that directive means, or implies, that she is, in some way, apart? For God's sake, she thinks, just get up and go. The assumption that action dispels inertia readily enough is hardly the call of the wild. Chances are, once she bestirs herself, the utilitarian persona she has latterly adopted will do all the inglorious rest. Then this uncharacteristic hiccup in her preferred etiquette will be forced to retreat back to from whence it came. Whether that whence will ever be investigated again is purely what remains to be seen.

God, fatigued now by the chatter within and at last resolved, she stands to expedite the plan. Joints and spine and muscles, up! There it is, dark parquet firmly underfoot. High thread-count sheets let fall from her grip. Room viewed from a little above. She does not even glance around and steps into her decision purposefully now. Then . . . takes a detour to the window on the far side of the room. Her footfalls muted by the rug. Drapes obscuring the view beyond. Over there the shards grown whiter and long reveal the pelmet is dusty, and badly hung. She can see it even better now and how the too vigorous might easily, accidentally, pull it down. She considers if more light might wake him up. That'd be one way to bring a resolution about. Probably not the simplest but . . . She tugs hard on the cord anyway.

Day.

Unspectacular and only again. Blind spinning on

its roller. Another curtain undrawn. Irrefutably another night spent in a similar room to the one for which she has paid. Handsomely. Enough. Her presence in this morning's room is something of an aberration and certainly no longer the a.m.'s expected jump-cut whenever she is far from . . . home. Fog on the glass. She touches that and its cold shoots a fern up her arm. Flesh and bone cannot be fooled. She's journeyed far from the building blocks of youth, and need make no noise to ensure she's solid, so emits no audible response. At least this is what she thought until he turns behind her in his sleep. In his bed. She twists to the sound and sees the chill on his back. But is her intuition about the cold right or is it only how this body hits this light? Rangily. Cadaverously. And might she be merely reconstructing a memory, one of many, from the time before? Here now finally is a thought which gives some meaning to her pause so she relinquishes her other diversions to further study him. There is something in his breathing out and breathing in. What exactly remains unclear and she is relieved there's no need for an immediate answer, were there even someone to ask. There are only the two of them in this room and he, despite the warning turn, is still far off in sleep. But even were he wide awake, he'd know nothing of that life or have cause to take an interest in it. How either arrived in this transitive place is

68

irrelevant to the subsequent acquaintance they made. Her order of tea at the bar while rubbing heat back into her hands. His suggestion of a brandy which she gratefully declined – after all it's not winter yet. Something lighter then? A glass of wine perhaps? From this simple crossing they had proceeded to the odd joke parried. All suspicions dispelled by their increasingly nimble chat and a quick-found shared interest or two. Nothing of greater import has passed between then and now and everyone probably knows everyone's name. Nice to keep the knife-edge nowhere in sight. She appreciates the pleasanter hygiene of it. It's just how the cold looked on the skin of his back which caught her slightly off guard. She knows she can rally beyond it, although she might also fall in. It seems, briefly, so likely she takes the preparatory breath. Closes her eyes. Memory assembles. Then she refuses to collaborate. There was a time before she knew how to do that but she can't really recall now how she managed it. Youth, probably. And it's not that the past hasn't earned its weight, its weight just never helps with the pull.

On that sobering note, she turns to the window again. The city palpable, if enigmatised, by the condensation. Undeniably there has been some breach though, through which all of these questions now begin to pour, unluckily for her. Why is it better to stand in his room? And why better at his window than door? She knows it's not a matter of dreading the time after this. It invariably arrives and she's rarely not welcomed it. So, this demurral is not forestalling that. On the contrary, it's comforting to still find this odd: the inexact ebb between knowing someone and forgetting again. Besides – and not to further distract herself but – if she breathes onto the glass and carefully wipes, she can see to the fjord. To the promenade. To the opera house. To a damp sky beyond weakening into day. Not very beautifully, she thinks – although liking, as always of late, a high-up view of the streets. Of people too, who perhaps also don't admire it. Of people starting to dress for the cold. Of people at tram stops. Of people crossing roads into buildings for what she supposes are about to become their working days. Where she can't see, she imagines workstations and desks, up to which people will catch lifts or climb the stairs. There'll be hooks or castored chairs where they'll dump their coats. Laptops they'll carelessly prise open, maybe bowing their heads to log on? But before they sit, they'll fetch a coffee – if that's what Norwegians like? At tea stations, fill their mugs while swapping some life – did you see that thing or hear about this? Perhaps books – noir, she hopes. Probably sport. Some local outrage or international disgrace. Politics. Europe. TV.

The United States. Like all of this will forever be and invariably begin again. She envies their faith that the future continues to be approaching them. She has long since ceased living that way. Yet she remembers the certainty she and he once possessed of possessing no enemy but Time. Sat on the couch with her legs over his, reading the paper as he smoked a cigarette. His long fingers through hers making knots on their quilt. Laid on cut grass with her head next to his. The rain running all down his face. No.

Stop.

Turn.

She should and should not think of this. If the past comes in it will wring her neck. So, she prevails upon her memory to recollect it as though from far away. And it is far away. Now, very far away. Perhaps a little far. All the Chinese takeaways eaten or pairs of shoes bought in the years from then to here. What a poor choice of gauges. She doesn't even like Chinese anymore, it's just what they often ate together. And she knows perfectly well she has never gone unshod but if asked she could not describe a single shoe. Not offhand. Not right now. But she refuses to give up. Blue. More likely black. Some with heels. Boots probably – she does have a fondness for those. His she could summon up more easily, from that last time when she picked them out for him. Black leather with a good-as-new lace. She'd been there when he bought them, on her exhortation. 'For God's sake,' she had said as they passed the shop. 'Just go in and get a new pair right now, you've almost walked yours through.' The look on his face at her imperative tone and the laughter wreaking havoc round his eyes. Then he'd capitulated with 'I don't want to be a source of shame!' and then he . . . And then she had followed him in. Men's shoes, the eternally worst kind of dull. She suspects he bought the first pair upon which his eyes fell. But they were fine, they were plain and would do. Also, he was happy enough to wear them out and leave the old ones for the bin. 'Satisfied?' he'd enquired, back out on the street. Ignoring his obvious tongue in cheek, she indicated she was and knew he was pleased and then they walked for ages despite the heat but he didn't getmuchmoreuseoutofthem . . . As for his love of a Singapore fried noodle? It didn't matter then. It certainly doesn't in here. Christ, memory. What is the purpose of remembering that?

And so, it comes. Anyway. She pushes it back. She is certain she hasn't made a sound but then, from behind, the stranger turns again. She holds still, deathly so. Every muscle alert to the disaster which seems to be imminent now, should he open his eyes, should he see this look on her face. Not that he has any possible context through which to read what it means, it's just . . . she'd rather he did not. He'd rather he did not or flounder around in an abortive effort. She works to organise her expression. He deeply breathes. She wills the emotion roving her face to congeal back into repose. There is a dicey moment. There is the next dicey moment. He breathes again. And then it is gone. His back might be cold but enough of him's warm to remain disinclined to wake up.

Breathe yourself.

Turn and go.

Why don't you? Why aren't you already gone? You should. It will be time for breakfast soon. Doubtless far below hotel kitchens churn so, while he remains unconscious, she should make her way now and go back down to her room. Besides, isn't it always preferable to be decent, were they later to chance-meet in the lobby or dining room, even in the lift? She wasn't listening when he mentioned the duration of his visit. She was just deciding she would. Perhaps he was too because he didn't seem unduly concerned by her fleeting lapse in attention, the way the touchy get. That's also how she knew no trouble was afoot. Transactionally, they were evenly pitted. Both – or so it seemed to her – equally willing to do or do without. Uncanny, all things considered now, his favouring the same unsentimental directness she does and his correct assumption of how this approach would suit her fine. Well, well, this must be who she is. Or who she presents to be read. Or else it all just fell into place because . . . he resembled who he did.

Yes.

Now she thinks of it, as he watched her rub the heat back in through her fingers it may have briefly crossed her mind. Some fleeting similarity caught out of the corner of her eye. But no, that can't be right. That would be so appallingly trite. It was only his back, just now. Or was it? It's almost funny how last night she failed to notice it. Wilfully? No, presumably she was just preoccupied with everything else: the drinking of drinks, the lighting of cigarettes, the ongoing sub-conversational assessment. This morning though, it's so obvious. And this is why she cannot leave. Damn. This is the reason and knowing it now cannot be undone. But is it so wrong to play looking at him again? I mean, I do know it isn't him. It isn't even a very good impersonation. Just blue light falling over hollow ribs, pale skin and how his hair falls on the bone of his cheek. Older too than he was . . . but not than he would have been. I'm only looking now. And I miss him. And the part of me that thought I would never learn to live without.

Turn and look at the sky instead. Look and envy it. Brightening now and fading grey-white as far as the eye can see. As far as her eyes can see. Her eyes can see so far.

He turns too, yet again. It's almost a signal that she is cutting it too fine. He must be so close to waking now. Not that she doubts he would be alright. She imagines he'd be as ambivalent about finding her gone as finding her by his side. She thinks he'll probably say his good mornings, stretch and rub his eyes. He may even insist on ordering room service to be polite. Unless she's been very much mistaken, he is the type and there's nothing at all wrong with that. But his courtesy, his directness, even his fastidiousness in bed – not fastidious pernickety, it's just the world stayed on its axis. It was alright though. She has no complaints. A good job was done and . . . never mind – these are not the reasons why she is still here. She'd rather she could continue having no idea why she is still here but that would not be true. So, she allows herself to be what she is and permits herself another look at his back, his ribs and the dawn light on his hair. She is not really seeing what it is she longs to see again. She's seeing something though. An artist's impression. Seeing enough to help her pass through this awful moment of longing and on into the safer next. Sometimes, she thinks, there are rewards which accompany this occasionally not seeing clear.

But – and she swears this is her final digression – if she just stayed until he woke and said, 'Good morning,' what might happen?

Something intimate?

Something pleasant?

Maybe something more?

No.

And a resounding no.

I do not belong here now.

I do not belong here anymore.

So.

She turns her gaze back to the window and into the ineffectual dawn, as a city she scarcely knows begins to do what it wants. She bears it no ill will but can't arouse in herself the slightest interest in whatever that might be. Instead, she touches the cold glass once more and once more feels the fern. It's good to know, despite all that's passed this hour, she has a body still affected by the world. Then far north, above, a gull passes aslant, grey-white in the grey whitening up into light. Another. Another. And another after it. Discrete in themselves but perhaps loosely a flock. She watches as a current

guides and carries them further off to where, she supposes, lies the sea. From all that way up there what can
they see? And if she were to listen carefully would she
hear the sound they make?

*Birmingham*

*Stansted*

*Sligo*

*Leigh*

*Enniskillen*

*Birmingham*

*Edinburgh*

*Paris*

*New York*

*Worcester MA*

*New York*

*Princeton*

*Ostuni*

*Bristol*

*Bristol*

*Birmingham*

*Cork*

*Jerusalem*

*Amsterdam*

*Den Bosch*

*Beijing*

*Chengdu*

*Suzhou*

*Shanghai* x

*Toulouse*

*New York* x

*Edinburgh*

*Auckland*

It is the farthest furthest she has ever been. On a flat earth she would be at the edge. As it is, to go on might be the shortest way home and just let the world fold back on itself. For despite some perplexity regarding her current notions of home – and her periodic declarations that that is simply not so – her belief in the planet's curve is secure. It is an unbreachable line, and one of the few of which she has ever been sure. Until now, here, in this outermost place. As the ground imperceptibly spins beneath and all around her the heavens shift, she finds herself thinking she wouldn't object to some more tangible proof it exists. Out there somewhere, she knows is the ocean and horizon, with nothing to be seen after it. She can't help envisaging – admittedly, flying in the face of all sense – a great cataract roiling at the deep sea's end towards which she, and New Zealand, inexorably inch. Torn from or flowing to, to be dragged over the edge and churned into particles of dust, or particles of time, or whatever becomes of a body once it has attained its finest grade of dismemberment.

This may all be a touch cataclysmic, she will admit, especially as on her arrival it was already night so she has no idea what it looks like out there. That said, in terms of proof, she's not asking for much – mathematical calculations or satellite photographs. No, really just a physical hint. Some readily appreciable sensation for instance. Say, how toes inevitably touch the ground after heels in a continuous, predictably repeating sequence? Of course, she understands there may be disparities within this pattern too. As far as walking goes however, it is the expected usual and in her general indifference to personalised nuance she does not feel she has been remiss because . . . because who thinks about every step? Well, there are some people who obviously must but, having been fortunate with her health, she does not number herself among them. She wouldn't even think of it now except it seems the ground has somehow misplaced her confidence in it. Either that or – and this would be considerably more abstract – the soles of her feet have begun doubting themselves.

Is it an actual possibility that such a precisely located doubt might exist? She is inclined to think it is not. Realistically, she must presume, her feet may have a problem afoot. It's quite rare for the ground to change itself. Highly unlikely over the course of an average ride in a lift, and all was still well back on the ground floor. Although she realises this is an earthquake zone, she has had experience of tremors on her travels before and this is not like that. What exactly it *is* like, however, is proving harder to nail down. But something was clearly amiss from the moment its trundle ground to a halt and she stepped out onto her given floor. As though there was a suddenly insufficient amount of air, or gravity had ceased to be non-negotiable. Not, of course, affecting everything – there were no floating occasional tables or independently occurring asphyxiations to be witnessed. No, it appeared to be her alone forced to gingerly navigate the over-lit corridor. Providentially her room lay directly across but, for all the three or four steps it took, her faith in the immutability of bricks and mortar has taken a significant knock.

She's not terrifically keen on how this makes her brain look so it may, ultimately, prove preferable to lay these complications at her feet. And why shouldn't she? They currently reside at ground zero of the issue – her arms are feeling fine. Even so, an unambiguous description of the problem is hard to get across. Her best guess, her best explanation is . . . they – her overly animate feet – fear taking another step. They seem to suspect they'll find themselves in an empty place and then, on stepping back, step back into no place where everything expected is gone. A sort of waking version of sleep's ever surprising jolt into a deeper down. Rationally she knows, even as she only reflexively reflects, this fear is incredibly cogent, especially for feet. But to be frank, she's too tired to be operating at full speed. Her mind will have to take her body's word for it and, from where she is standing now, she really believes it. In truth, she daren't take one more step. Then she takes one, to thwart her predilection for the melodramatic. She doesn't take another one though.

Instead, she casts her eyes across the room. From the ridged cream wallpaper past the wall-mounted screen, over the gold sheen of the bedspread to the open blind window, to the night and the city beyond. Twinkle twinkle there you are, a solitary life on an anomalous star – or planet, as the case may be. Beige carpet matched to the dark brown skirting. But her preoccupation with the decor has never been less specific. The details lie on the top of her brain and will not be admitted. There have been more hotel rooms than she will ever care to think of. Now she is looking for something else and she searches for what it is.

Then.

Too much ado, far too much ado about nothing, she curtly reflects.

It's not inconceivable either a recovered sense of perspective might be the extent of it, making this palaver a mere spell of jitters, consistent with a parching twenty-four-hour flight. Or even, perhaps, that weird gold hutch of a lift?

Well indeed, there is that.

She's never been particularly claustrophobic but finds herself already shuddering to think of it. A box of reflections closing in. And, while she has frequently seen that very same design before, the three hundred and sixty degrees of mirror have rarely induced more alarm. Front, back and either side on, there was no escaping the persistently receding self-contemplation, especially of her face. Perpetual cheekbones and eyes sunk under yellow light – designed perhaps by fans of a vague touch of jaundice? That same thought had occurred, and tickled her, in there but she hadn't laughed aloud because of the engrossed blusher application of the woman on the other side. And by 'engrossed' she means there had been an unreasonably 'do or die' quality to the putting on, but then, she shouldn't judge. For all she knows perhaps it was. After all, isn't female skeletonisation now just a shorthand for 'loved'? Or is that 'lovable'? She doubts death was truly in the air though, not for that consternated face, so she is going to judge anyway. Or would, if she could be bothered and she can't tonight. They're your cheeks, stranger, so do what you like. All these faces mean nothing to me and yours isn't even the most interesting in this lift. That prize goes to his expression of exquisite suffering while also smothering a laugh. She'd first heard it in his voice, then caught it in his eye. Then they played a quick game of I know that you know that I know that I no wait. She'll get to this strand later on.

First of all, she is thinking she knows flattery to be the intention behind such lights above mirrors. And she has already noticed this hotel to be frequented by those tormented by their need to look or, should that be, to be seen? But, from whichever perspective, only perfectly and unblemished by the glum accumulations of living. She envies what must be the relief of having only pre-occupations like that – while acknowledging they may not provide relief for those thus preoccupied. She wishes she could rub along with this attitude more ambiva-lently. Although that would require taking for granted the utter lack of value assigned to her many years of being alive. And she cannot buy in. She does not believe.

While she may not consider herself to have achieved any particular greatness in life, it's been hard enough to keep on clocking those decades up. To get to her late forties has taken a lot of ploughing through. There may have been considerable work put into forgetting too – sometimes with more success than she cares to admit – but without those accumulations displayed in plain sight it would be as if she had never lived at all. She'll not stoop to clichés about the blank canvas of youth – despite, generally, subscribing to their truth. She's just not unhappy about being a creature of oil and mess and stain. She has been bitten and will bite and there is a life in her home, even when she is not around, which bodily exists and is true.

But she doesn't want to think of that now.

This place is too remote and that place too far off.

Her intermittent agoraphobia flutters at the slightest mention of distance, even inside her head. As though on naming she might dematerialise into it. And, for the record, she doesn't appreciate the increasingly over-heated tone she has taken up. She much prefers herself when being rigorously pragmatic. To this end, she tells herself, everything back there is fine and her absence a mercy of not getting simple things wrong. Her existence a mercy of being alone and all the delight that entails.

So.

Hopping down from her high horse, she's now also inclined to confess that neither has she remained entirely immune to the fixations of her age. Not her personal age, naturally. That, she has embraced readily – recognising her luck – and never minded at all. If she cared about her face, she would call it beautiful and more now than twenty years ago. But she does not care. She will not opt in. She might even be willing to die on this hill. Forty-nine is as good as any place she could realistically be. Still too young for the truly great installations of regret. Too old for the game of being boored into silence. And if what-might-have-been does occasionally catch her out, well, no one gets everything. The net result is, those type of years have never been a cause of anxiety for her. By 'her age' she means simply her time, her era. This means there's a make-up bag in her bag. She possesses some kind of serum for her hair. She may even find herself dabbing something underneath her eyes later. And while deriding what erasure that copiously applied blusher might imply, neither did she just stare at the floor. For all her feigned obduracy she too looked in the mirror, albeit without feeling any pressure to improve what it was she saw there. But as she watched herself trying not to watch, she also saw herself stretch off into the void.

Infinitely.

Meaninglessly.

And, if she elected to never move again, eternally.

Forever the carnival trick of a seeing woman trying not to see? Forever the carnival trick of a woman trying not to be . . . opened into every room on every floor in every hotel around the world? Unfolded and unfolded, boundlessly. Never to be less or more, better or worse. Just this crystallised extending version of self. Liberated from the scourge of accountability as well as hope of reprieve. But no . . . not exempt reality. Still moving forward. Still on the inside of time. And, actually, is she about to become the carnival trick of a high-rise woman who . . .

Christ!

Again?

Stop that!

Do not move. Do not take a step and *do not* go over there.

No.

So . . .

Instead?

What an incredibly morbid cast of mind, she thinks. Most likely too to be erroneous, based, as it is, on the supposition that every room in this place – as well as everywhere else – is the same and the same and the same. She knows that cannot possibly be true. There have been no significant social movements crying out for the democratisation of hotel rooms – not that she's been privy to anyway. So, an empiricist when she wants to be – and that time should be now – she then admits it, candidly. Not all hotels are created equal. Therefore, what happens within their rooms cannot be identical and she has absolutely not just been killing time. Killing it until when?

No!

Have you not been listening to yourself?

Not that!

No!

Hotels.

Oh yes.

Some must have bigger bathrooms. Super king beds. Perhaps facilities more elaborate than a teabag and kettle, or a dispiritingly understocked mini-bar – she's not reflecting on her own room's amenities now, she has yet to check. But opportunities for increased billing and superfluities aside, she will not, cannot deny that, once distilled all hotel rooms are essentially alike, if not exactly the same. A place built for people living in a time out of time – out of their own time anyway. And if that isn't always the reason why they came, it is often the reason she has.

She really doesn't want to start with all that.

It's a fundamentally impractical use of her time and, ultimately, these maunderings cast little light on the situation with her floor.

She notes that she now finds it preferable to designate it as 'a floor situation' rather than any difficulty with her body which – despite her best efforts – continues mainly to exhibit strength and provide no tangible reason for doubt. And why should she seek to doubt it? After all, it's hers. Also, her feet are clearly there, inside her shoes, and visible against the abstract shag-pile swirls. When she flexes their muscles, they instantly move. Their look, and their function, is perfectly fine. It's just . . . What? She has lingering concerns about whether anything exists beneath what she is standing on. And, let's face it, there's nothing like the threat of the abyss to make one reluctant about purposefully striding across an unfamiliar floor.

Which is utter nonsense, she immediately scoffs.

Then immediately asks what's holding her body up?

Not time anymore.

And what about her feet?

Stop.

She knows there is no real logic to this. For God's sake she has just, literally, ceased to contrast the potential contents of the other rooms. She knows they are below. They are actually there. She knows too, beneath this carpet lies a floor. Wood. Some kind of cement.

Steel beams. Wiring and fittings from which light fittings can be suspended. Then exactly the same below that again, over and over, right the way down. There will be, *will* be basements, carparks, foundations, rock and plenty more between there and the centre of the earth. She cannot fall through or find herself accidentally returned to the place from which it has taken her so long to arrive. There is no going back. There is only on. And, furthermore, there is nothing malign at work. The laws of physics have not been disturbed in order to give her a scare. And why would the laws of physics ever consider her to be in need of one? She's scarcely an inflection on the flabbergasting spectrum of life, not to mention just one of many human beings tonight who have found themselves on this sixth floor. The powers that be – should they exist, and they do not – need take no notice of her. She is doing fine. Very well. Yes, she is tired so she is not quite herself. Or she is herself and the problem is worse than she thinks. Maybe even the worst there is? Stop this.

Stop again.

She recovers herself. She is recovered from her existential overindulgence. In summation, she is not alone in opposition to some malevolent grand design – even if in low moments it has felt like that. The universe is not conscious and therefore has no idea she exists. She has, of late, preferred it like this – when she has been bothered to prefer.

Better.

Better and more like herself.

And now she has arrived at the moment to push the whole way through. Which means it's precisely the wrong moment for drawing attention to what else she'd been considering back in the lift. Which was what? What time is it? No, not . . . No. Pushing the whole way through doesn't involve thinking of that. To go on is to keep going on.

So, to this end.

She puts down her bag. She closes the door. Nothing happens. Her hand relaxes and she is alone now. She throws her key card on the writing desk. She removes her coat. She lies it lengthwise on the bed. An extensive array of physical movements are made and all without consequence. There is, manifestly, no true cause for alarm. If there seem to be a thousand angled lamps blazing that's usual enough, as will be the ritual later tonight of learning which switch is which. And isn't there a volcano here somewhere? she cribs from the back of her mind or maybe the in-flight magazine of the airline. Dormant now, she remembers, unfortunately. She's keen to see the crater anyway – she appreciates a good chasm into which she can stare. But on facing the window and administering her paranoid jetlag a slap in the face, the only sight to be seen is herself.

A ghost in the glass.

Her inclination, once more, for the dramatic.

Even so, a ghost in the glass.

The impression remains.

It's the kind of thing could overwhelm her with spectral remembrance if she hadn't inhabited her own absence before. The vacated place. She knows it exists; she'd just rather avoid it.

Then the weight makes it fall anyway.

Tube rides where her silent grief was so palpable, strangers, unbidden, rose and offered their seats. And she'd slipped into them staring past the hems of coats to the tunnel-blind window across – that pained replication of her white face constructing windows to remembering too. Remembering all the times he'd sat with her on the same tubes. Slouched. Faces facing their reflection-drained looks and remembering. Apparently, this is her memory's set-piece from their hard times – enshrined as such, probably, because of the motion and silence public transport can enforce. Or perhaps she's endowing it retroactively? But, given memory can produce proof they laughed on the underground plenty, why would she do that? Because lately going anywhere, except on foot, translates to a kind of despair. No.

That actually wasn't a question.

Well the response, if not answer then, still remains a No.

This is another argument she cannot win so returns herself to remembering them, sitting ghostly on their long-ago trains, remembering in their bad times, their good. She will remember too they were sometimes unsure. Sometimes they looked from themselves to the fraughtly loved other and did not know what was coming next. Just as she remembers that the city moving above their heads did not help at all. Its business was purely providing routes of escape. She remembers when they did and did not take them. She remembers, in her early grief, wishing to go back to that static place and see him in it again. See him in that hardship too – feeling it while still sitting next to her though. Ghosts in the glass but at least as two. Not a ghost in the glass remembering all the ghosts that have been. And now here, a ghost again. Also alone but not the same. Stationary rather than on a train. And not as crippled as she had been then. Not irradiated by pain. Not irradiated now, she'd say, by anything. Cool and calm. Cool and calm, if not for her irk with the floor.

Oh, not that again.

She should marshal beyond it.

She usually can.

These little things that drag you down – what you would, if you could, amputate.

Cut.

She takes off her scarf. She even hangs it up. She wishes the hotelier's fondness for light sources had not been quite so profligate. She's come a long way, after all. She'd like to look unimpeded, from the window and, most specifically, past her own gloom. In truth she knows she easily can. Just walk to where she's long clocked the control dial. She can simply dim the lights down or even switch them off. It's an elementary solution which requires no convincing herself of. So, she does. She can. She does just that. Steps forward onto the fine firm unflinching floor. Grips tight, then turns the button. Sees the glare definitively go and her own unwelcome outline fade. But in the spotlights' stead, the remnants of her body are now invaded by the avid lighting out in the street. How bright it is, big city New Zealand. Precisely how big she does not yet know. But at the flick of a switch it has become a great deal more prominent and she has receded again. Now pierced red in hand, in head and breast. A wrong-sexed St Sebastian skewered beside a dormant volcano. No one will be making any art films about her.

Look further though.

She does.

But, in the untraversable glass, what she sees is the city become part of herself although she is not part of it. Her entire image shot through by its very least effort. She bridles with aggravation at the rank unfairness. For, whatever the tricks of this lighting and however banal this thought, this moment sits lucidly inside her now – meaning a specific recollection of it has been made. A grand memory of isolation, randomly illuminated, then screwed into the vegetal bolts of her brain. So now, at any arbitrary time, she will be compelled to bear its resurfacing. Despite not wanting to, she will know again the many ways she is displaced from where she once unthinkingly dwelled. Some might think that cruel. Others, that's life. She: how to cannily arm oneself against it, as well as its backhand inducement to wanting again, or not? She has no firm opinion yet. And, really, it's too little a matter to inspire such vehement distaste. After all, it will be just another memory of another place in which she is still just her. Only the 'unmanageability of want' might be of concern, if she could raise the necessary ire. She already knows she will not. Want is a place she now very rarely inhabits, beyond habitually. And rousing ire requires so much effort that expending it tends to leave her embarrassed. Who cares about her ire anyway?

Or about her anyway?

Or anyway generally?

Who cares?

Go on, say it!

Nihilist!

Yeah . . .

What she would like is to lie down and go to sleep. Perhaps later order room service and watch TV. Then feel her body give in to the bed. Allow her brain to succumb to the jetlag as though she'll never have to get up. She should have a shower. She knows that but, taking comfort in the seal of her post-travel grime, is unwilling to let it go. It will keep her in nowhere and on the right side of choice. She will think about making one but will not because, before anything, she should wash and if she hasn't done that . . . then what can she possibly do?

It is a way to keep hold.

It is a method of crowd control.

A sleight of hand.

A diversion.

Even a moat.

An informal abdication from the corporeal world.

One of many ways not to exist.

Also, easier to backtrack from than putting on weight, although that too has had its time and use.

You see, there are a great many doors to which she has applied her knuckles.

Because.

Sometimes she does not know what to do . . . or how to do better than that.

Anyway.

It's fine.

There really is no need for this fuss.

Well, you're the only one here, so . . .

I know . . . give it up.

Remember where you are and look out!

It's a city!

Look!

Remember when you were young? Remember your rapacity before him, or any of them, when all you wanted to do was see? And you never thought you wouldn't be free? And you still don't really think you're not. You have just become . . . not that bothered. Because you apparently think you've had enough. Not in any terminal way. More in the way in which . . . you have arrived at this remotest place and are mostly interested in decoding oblique directives from your feet or lying on that preposterously upholstered bed eating chips? That's not very good. Is it even true? Look out the window. Properly. Rouse yourself to it. Know how very far away you are.

I do know.

I know how far.

And?

It's not that. It's where I've reached.

But she does look out the window properly.

Now go close up.

This, she also does.

A sharp spur of anxiety runs up her leg. She dismisses it. She knows it is all in her head. If only she could get a good look outside, she might better locate herself in relation to the volcano. To the city. This island. Or – dramatically – *to the world*. But, bathos aside, she still can't – see very clearly, that is. She'll have to wait. What's the time now? And what's the time difference anyhow? There's no way she can smoke in here.

The spur again. Now coming on strong. It might just be stress. Most probably brought on by hours of breathing recycled air. She really wouldn't mind having it a bit fresher in here. She pushes on the window. It won't budge. She searches its frame for a means to unlock but . . . there is no option for it. This idea is going nowhere. Shift away from this. Shift away.

Before she can she'd like a plausible cause for the foot thing, to put it to bed. Maybe it's the glass itself, inciting some preconscious desire for flight? Or a rare physical manifestation of that common dream from childhood? No, she remains unconvinced by this take. And besides, for God's sake, when has she ever been the earthbound type? Even the span of her vertigo was brief or – more accurately – quite a long time ago. She has always been in love with concrete, and daffodils be damned. She doesn't care anymore when her feet aren't on solid ground. And if she doesn't particularly like those hours in the air? Well, she's flown enough to know that being Schrödinger's traveller, especially over vast distances, can wreak havoc on good sense. Without doubt too, the dying-off sound of strange birds outside doesn't particularly help. It's like they're torturing dinosaurs out there. If she went out into it what would happen to her?

Nothing.

Because nothing is going to happen to her.

Besides . . .

She is not going to go out.

There have been enough thresholds crossed today. More would be making a meal out of it. No, at best, she will stay in this room worrying that something is really wrong but paralysing her every impulse to action with arguments she can neither win nor lose. Apparently, she likes circles. She hopes she does because she's been living within them for ages now. Chasing her mind and body around in a herculean effort to undermine every gasp for oxygen. Something of a platitude but also true. Nowadays it's all back to the wall and eye on the door, or window – more accurately – as of fifteen minutes ago. But she requires of herself that she will make peace with this room. She may even order up some wine to rub the edges off her self-diagnosing. Unusual sensations in the feet can prove to be a serious symptom of . . . She knows. She will not look it up. That way lies madness and she is already sufficiently conversant with driving herself out of her mind. Besides, her feet are fine. Fine is the floor. Fine her fine miser's brain as it flips over its haul of all the fine things that might make fine things more fine.

For instance: the room number of the man with whom she shared the car in. How, at the front desk, he'd repeated it, pretending it was not for her benefit. How he'd mentioned that around eight he'd probably head down to the bar. Have a Scotch or two, to help him unwind. And what his not saying 'whiskey' implied. You see? There it is. But why is she remembering it like this? Like clues instead of how, on stepping into the lift, he'd pleasantly asked if, perhaps later, he could buy her a drink? Or if she'd rather, maybe grab something to eat? He allowed that everyone's remedy for jetlag is different but they're both here in this far-flung hotel for the duration . . . so . . . why not?

And then the lift doors shut.

And she gazed at the woman opposite vigorously making up.

And at the yellow light on his face.

And into the thought of the night.

And how much younger he seemed now than in the cab.

And how age doesn't matter.

And who cares about the gap?

And herself in the mirror.

And herself reflecting back.

And the secret paralytic of the whole event, what lay hidden behind everything else: Tomorrow I will be older than you, for the first time. I am about to pass you by. After all these years, and how it always was, the time where that shape kept its shape has almost run out. You will stay behind now and become younger than me. And I have come so far to escape this but the hours are quickly catching up. They must be halfway across the world by now so there is no more time. There is only the edge and this little while is all our old balance has left. If I could just look back and look back and never change, would I choose that for myself?

And then the man in the lift reiterates: so why not?

And she cannot think.

She can't decide.

I might see you down there later, she smiles.

Then does not think of it again because the doors slide apart and she finds her feet are unwilling to go forward.

She makes them though.

And makes herself.

And hears the doors close behind.

And knows he goes upwards.

And feels her body want to open, and not.

And now she is here.

So.

Time is all there is.

And knowing which part she would rather play, she looks at the impervious window, yawns, and asks herself if she really has the energy for this? Hasn't she already decided she's tired of herself and pretty much of everyone else? But it's her birthday tomorrow so, perhaps, she should just lighten up? Get in the shower. Have a good wash. Recognise the world's end isn't over the horizon. Stop pretending there's anything wrong with her feet.

Or the fucking floor.

She should . . .

She should . . . by now . . . she should know what to do.

And then she does.

She will look out that window in the morning. She will orientate herself. She will admire the volcano or whatever of it is left. And then she will watch boats sail back in from the farthest-off point of the sea. She will bite down. She will continue on, willingly. Willingly. It's annoying because she has created this version already. She just occasionally lets it slip.

*Sydney* x

*Brisbane*

*Melbourne*

*Canberra*

*Dublin*

*Bath*

*Bristol*

*Charleston*

*Oxford*

*Cheltenham*

*Liverpool*

*Manchester*

*Vancouver*

*Washington DC*

*New York*

*Portland OR*

*Austin* x

She opens the door. He says, 'Can I come in?' She closes the door again. He manages a 'Hold on!' before it shuts but she, weightless in the width of shock, replaces the chain and turns the lock then listens for his footfalls away. Upon hearing none, she admits harbouring some doubt that she would. So now, although she cannot be certain, she may reasonably deduce he is devising an alternative approach. She already knows she's miscalculated the outcome of this and, given her natural antipathy towards inconclusiveness, is irritated by having gotten it wrong. Also, and almost worse, where is the unrufflable demeanour she's so painstakingly constructed? She'd appreciate it reasserting itself now.

This angst is pointless though, and wasteful too.

Take a breath.

Wait a beat.

Self-reproach is a luxury for which she, manifestly, does not have the time.

She really ought to be getting on with spreading the logic around.

An untender resolve now is, obviously, all. Settle on the parameters of the decision then make the choice. Even the wrong one would be preferable to this stalled botch. And if the scale of it appears unmanageable, just start small. Compartmentalise. She is already accomplished in this department after all and may rely on it to stand her in good stead.

So.

Should she spy through the spyhole? She has little stomach for that: the queasy fish-eyed reflection of her own anxious perspective. Also, she thinks she recalls a mention of his fondness for chess – not ostentatiously announced but in reference to something else – so any such hackneyed move will have been anticipated, unquestionably. Perhaps he even banks on it? She can't really imagine why, although he has certainly gone very quiet out there. In fact, now the only sounds filtering through seem to issue from the housekeeping staff, beyond in the hall. Trolleys trundling, for instance. Distant discreet raps upon doors. Apologies in various Latin accents of whose particular origin she remains unsure. Why didn't she study Spanish in school? Well . . . because there was only French and even the French teacher had appeared unenthusiastic about imparting it. Never mind. It was the tenses she could never quite get. Never mind. And numbers above sixty, who can keep track of all that? Never mind. The education system isn't on trial. Never mind. It doesn't matter. She's here now so . . . think. What is the reaction he might not expect? Well, and she realises this is weak but in her graceless desperation it's something at least and in this way a decision gets made.

So.

To thwart whatever advantage he imagines he's gained by his intemperate, unwarranted, over-zealous display, she definitively turns her back on the spyhole and presses her spine to the wood. She is aware, as a countermove, this isn't much use but in light of the previous paralysis its impact is enormous. She can finally approve breathing out. And does. And looks around. Not a great deal of this room rejoins her to calm. She persists however until a quiet confidence arrives that she might – if only at some obtuse angle – have regained the upper hand. And if he doesn't realise she has? Well, surely that's just greater proof? Take your triumphs where you find them, she thinks, especially when the thick of battle appears to be your only alternative. A little melodramatic perhaps but she gets her own point and therefore lets the time slow down. Sheathes the panic back under her skin. Becomes a little more of herself again and lets the room be what it is.

Cool the wood behind her, though it stifles in here. She should switch the air conditioning on but if she moves from this area, this exact spot . . . actually, what will occur? Hardly all hell break loose – that's merely the impression she seems most comfortable with. And if she knows herself, as she thinks she does, she must admit the reasoning carries no weight. So, she really should turn it on. She can barely breathe and, in any event, the free flow of air is unlikely to impede her ability to think, or capacity to rationalise her way right out of this. Therefore, she marshals herself and mentally charts the course. The dial is over there, just around the corner. She pictures its approximate location in this blue L-shaped room. Yesterday it was the very first thing she had attended to – once she'd tossed her card key on the faux mahogany desk. It's on the wall somewhere . . . above her unpacked case . . . beneath the sealed PVC window. She need only take a few steps to make it to the other side of the bed. What could possibly be simpler than that? It's so easily accomplished. Of course, she can do this. She goes now to take the vital step but . . . oh . . . all her tendons are disinclined. Useless body! She'll hazard this is happening because it retains half an idea that he is still there, loitering in the corridor. It knows that just because she can't hear him out there, doesn't mean he's not patiently listening for her. Waiting for her to . . . what? Open the door? That mistake has already been made. Very obviously so. It is, in fact, what ensured her hopes of a seamless segue into being alone became absolutely kaput. God, she wishes she'd been more alert to his having had an ulterior motive but . . . what were the signs she missed? Too late, too late will be the cry, except she can't access enough moisture to dampen an eye, never mind allow tears to fall. This is insufferable, she thinks – in a bid to staunch the recriminatory eye-wincing – and Oh please come the afternoon.

Instead the air visibly heats beyond the glass as if the day is arming itself. She can't believe she turned the air conditioning off in the first place. It's not as though she's ever found this city cold. She's practically lived off its assuagements when she's been here before. When exactly was the last trip? A while ago. A year ago? She can't quite remember so tells herself that amid this chaos – but really, is it? – she can't trust herself to remember anything.

Although that's neither strictly nor loosely true.

The last time was a year and a half ago.

But since when is wishful thinking a crime?

And why should she remember?

Last time was just like this time.


Up until the point it was not.


Not this hotel but one like this. Hi and thanks and gone to bed and thanks and bye. In all ways consistent. She thinks he was American. She cannot be sure. Not from Texas, definitely. This accent she would remember. So, from somewhere else. And the tide mark of sweat on his shirt where he'd come in from the heat. Yes, she remembers it. American, in a white American shirt.

Very pleasant too. Entrance and exit, all passing off by the book. A perfect example, shining example of . . . what? How to live. She doesn't imagine she'll ever find herself recommending it but 'How to live' is accurate enough, as long as no further clarifications are sought. That particular enquiry desk is closed. You'll just have to make up your mind for yourself. Mine has already been made. Mind or bed? Oh, aren't you a screaming riot, the bloody black box in the head.

The intractable belligerence of this – her memory – is what she's come to hate. How it seems to insist on a future her past has already generated. No corrections. No deviations. Or, more concisely put: a coherent path for a conciliated self – for which she lacks sufficient new evidence to justify a change. She would have once – changed – practically on a whim. But that was before her hard-won victories over the excellent carnage of being young. Nowadays it's just being again, and always again, as you always were. In bleaker moments she wonders whether her very last choice has already been made? And, whatever her disillusion with this, she cannot deny there was a stage when that was exactly how she'd wanted it. Now seems to be the time when she has finally grown tired of it: this entombment in more practical, replicable versions of herself, erected on the notion that her past is a secret. And it isn't a secret. It just became the easiest version to be.

Oh he, the now long lost, wouldn't approve if he knew. If he knew? This beats all. He doesn't know. He doesn't know anything anymore and hasn't now for years. Stop that! Too brutal, she recoveringly thinks – and whenever this specific thought combusts, her remorse is immediate. It's a subtraction too close to be endured because in the molecules he left behind, which have enabled her to keep going, he is still alive. Molecules though? For God's sake, who says that? Since when has she thought 'Molecules' an acceptable way to describe . . . describe what? No, don't start playing semantics with yourself when you know full well what you mean. And she does. So – if somewhat warily – she says it then; the place in which he is still alive is their only child. His solitary son. The person from whom she has most tried to run, and to never run.

How do you like them apples? Not so very much. But in a long world of unanswered whys the explanation behind this statement is, in many ways, clear. Relatively. And it seems to be: she has at times, perhaps frequently, found it harder to stare at that life than that death. Now would be an excellent moment to stop because ah ah ah death again. Only a word until it's actually said. Then it strikes itself hard off both sides of the well, right down, all the way to the splash. But this is veering off at an angle, she knows, and therefore will not do. She's far too keen to sit in her palace and make all the words, arrange them at whim then ultimately discover herself wondering what the hell is going on? So, she returns to 'running' and 'tried to run'. Whereto is clear. Also, when. This appears to mean her suspiciously generalised thesis is: There's a cruelty to watching the living live once intimately possessed of the verifiable evidence that all life comes to an end. That it can be suddenly, and at any time, stopped. Be shorn from any body. Leave any onlookers bereft and apprehensive ever after about the possibility of also . . . or again. Then trying not to but not knowing how not to because she has been changed.

Oh.

God.

Not that.

She refuses it.

She shakes it off.

She knows so much about these assaults and yet, seemingly, still cannot resist.

She scans her body for some distracting wound to press but it's pretty well; even her mouth is not, currently, in need of a dentist. Her skin, despite her revels, bears not the slightest nick. Her shoes may be nondescript but fit so she has no grazes or blisters to attack. In short, she possesses no immediate means by which to hurt herself back into the clear. How she longs for that sky to be blue. But, ideologically opposed to her own despair, she contemplates a heavy blow to the wall instead. And the ameliorating effects of such an activity are: the gratifying click and bruise of knuckles. The pain shooting its ferns up into her arm. The slightly amazed exhalation, then the clarity behind. All very tempting, yet she does not permit herself this. There remains the matter beyond the door, and only with careful deliberation will she ensure it becomes appropriately resolved.

Yes.

More of that.

So.

While she may be sufficiently superstitious to think dwelling on death has the potential to curse, she has no intention of allowing that to determine her slightest move. She will think about whatever she likes. Whenever!

Better!

And now to revert to a dependable groove. On this occasion the 'obdurate atheist' she keeps well prepared should do. It works like a clean bill of health – if a clean bill of health is what you've sought in order to continue on as you were before. She knows this is roughly how it works for her and she's made all manner of peace with that.

Do.

Does.

And here she is.

Once ensconced safely within, she vetoes the intolerable self-justification in her tone. And why, in the first place, had she allowed herself to get as far as that? Carrying on as though her life was an isolated incident. As though no one else had ever experienced this, the human condition's most essential component: knowing someone alive, then knowing them dead. There. Done and dusted and yet . . . how much she felt it. How much she feels it. That much still remains true. Now as then. Now as when comforting their son on her knee. Now as him climbing in beside her, aged two or three, in the years just after, looking for him. Now as . . . now as . . . when the details mattered more. For instance, the how and when she first made the choice to look for who she had lost again, outside the region of dreams. Outside the ways she could remember him because the memories grew so thin that she didn't want to wear them out. So, she looked for him. She looked for him. And that state has fundamentally remained the same. She just decided, after a few false starts, not to take up residence in the hunt. Not to invest any more than the body in it and, even then, to spare no more than the moment. Afterwards, quick extraction has been key. There've been a few slips but this has been her way and she is sure their son will find his. He'll be an adult soon. Until he is, she'll remain vigilant about not rubbing his nose in it and has no reason to believe she ever has. After all, the search has never ended up in their home. Absolutely not in their bed. Never anywhere in London where he might chance to witness it. But in saying all that, which 'he' does she mean? Unfortunately for her, both, probably. This is also why, now that in a few years he'll leave home and has started expressing a wish for her to meet someone – she half suspects so she won't become a burden – she . . . she . . . doesn't know where to begin. Or how to begin. Or if to begin? Again.

It would be such a transgression, having been the very one she's so carefully abjured. Every occurrence to date has remained hers alone, and private. Even the men involved have never been privy to more – perhaps especially. To this end, she has made no promises. She has told no lies. One could – in the main – eat dinner off the manner in which she has conducted her sex life. Which makes her position here – back pressed to the door, in an Austin hotel – seem all the more unlucky. One might even say, undeserved. How can a single, and not unguarded, indiscretion have escalated to such a level – not to mention aroused within her this unseemly degree of dismay?

Although never a great advocate of apportioning blame, she will not permit herself to shy away from

asking why she has suddenly become so evidently careless as this. Reckless abandon may not have been it
but, obviously, it was something . . . troublesome . . .
and now something troublesome has dug in its heels.
And she is unaccustomed to it. Not that there haven't
been other moments when the outcome might have
been different, had she wanted it to be. Intermittently,
she has been tempted to make life face the other way.
Back on itself. Confronting again, just as she had in
the bewilder of being eighteen. Nineteen. Twenty. On.
But how on earth – given her then wide-ranging state
of confusion – had she managed that? With the aid of
youth's glorious absence of context . . . presumably.
And then, of course, soon enough she'd met him – the
perfect shoulder to cry at, the wall for her head to beat
against, but also the altitude to which all his afterbears
have yet failed to climb. She hates it but she knows it.
He was the thing and – although he was also certainly
his own type of challenge – that had been . . . that was
love . . . and she has never been enticed back to its bru-
talist mercies since.

Quite a bit to the contrary.

She's favoured the painless elegance of leaving all
those rooms, all those men. And if, in reality, it wasn't
all particularly elegant – especially earlier on – she had
at least ensured she invariably left alone. It hadn't come

naturally either, not double-checking their pleasure was pleased. And accustomed to the opposite as she had been, the perfect grade of disconnection had taken some time for her to correctly calibrate. She had mastered it though and settled in. She'd stopped lying to herself about what she was doing and grown so adept at a mode of unspoken invitation that she never after missed a chance. This had proved, as he had once described it himself, to be 'the knack' – a manner of looking at someone which guaranteed they would always look back. It had worked well for her, yielded up all the possible dividends, and, as it wasn't exactly nuclear fission, she'd never been much concerned with its toll. Why is it only now, long years after that chat, she suddenly recollects how he'd been unambiguous about it not being such a great trick to know? Not for him anyway, so he'd thought. But she doesn't think she's exploited it to the extent that he had. She's left no trail of half-consumed bodies strewn about. No broken hearts bleeding. No one feeling taken advantage of, or certainly not to any degree that might make her conscience prick. She's ready to swear there was never a single man left with any reason to expect an atom more than she gave. And she was liberal at night. Donated all to the cause. That was the deal. It was only in daylight that she never offered at all. Is that the truth? The whole truth? And nothing but the truth? So help her God, she still thinks it is. But . . . then . . . and in spite of all these prophylactics she'd considered set in stone, something has gone awry.

She stares into the carpet configurations beneath her feet. She imagines their purpose is to evoke Inca cities, or Aztecs. Her toes must wreak havoc on temples, or that is what she'd believe if she were a child again. She remembers it as a much-revisited game. Rendering big worlds from the small ones with which she could play. To those ants scuttling below me, do I seem to be God? Raising my hand against the sun, am I making their clouds? If I drop this stone, in this particular place, will it be the End of Days for them? And, when it occasionally crossed her mind, should I be cruel or kind? She opted for a radiant benevolence most of the time but whenever she chose to drop it, the second she saw it land, it became just a stone again. Those ants were just ants and she was just a girl with a completely clear conscience once more. When her real world grew, she let the game go – or so she had thought right up until . . . now. Which begs the question then, does she think of her life in these hotel rooms as laboratorially contained? Clearly the answer is yes, she has thought of it in that way. Each experience an experiment brought to culmination, data stripped, then labelled a failure or success. Is that really true? The answer is really yes:

anthill – hotel rooms, ants as men. On reflection she can't deny the similarities between these games and their, oh so conscientiously maintained, absences of consequence.

And now?

Does the ant bite back?

Is a real city to be rent in two?

Hardly.

There's not even a dent in the door. True, she's sweated into it like an invaded rampart but it remains structurally intact.

So, she summons the resources of her now decompartmentalised brain. There must be a fresh conclusion to be reached.

In the spirit of this, she breaks completely free. She turns back to the spyhole. She looks right through out of it and into the corridor. She sees him there, leant against the wall, picking the skin from a finger . . . waiting for her? Presumably he's hoping she will make some move. Perhaps undo the lock and open up? He hasn't pressed the bell again though. Chess or no chess, he doesn't know her well and can in no way be certain her actions are being reassessed, or even if she would? She could, after all, have just gone back to bed. Or be in the shower. Or calling down to have her laundry collected. He does glance towards the housekeeping staff now and then.

They give, and have, nothing to give away and, anyway, appear not to pay him the slightest heed. She imagines they've seen it all before. She thinks, however . . . God, the mess. And once more, how has it come to this? She doesn't know, but she knows if she thinks the likely cause will emerge. In the meantime, she refuses to panic again and instead attempts to re-access the intellectual pragmatism that's always served her best, before. In this precise moment, though, her palms only sweat too much and a rank incertitude reigns.

Decision. Indecision. Brain do your work. On her command then it flits over and back. It pinpoints her restlessness in this room last night. The jetlag and apathy at finding herself in yet one more anonymous hotel. The coffee didn't help. The thought of the bar below. Although she doesn't care for it, they might have a pianist at the piano? And it would do no harm to stretch her legs, especially after the length of that flight. Just the one then, she had decided, to help her wind down.

Avoiding the mirrors in the elevator. Avoiding her reflection in the door. Avoiding the eye of the pristine young soldier displaying medals across his chest. Ignoring the elderly couple thanking him for his service, and what she thought of that. The high, wide bar. The uneven spread of seats. She sat alone. The ivories tinkled. She inevitably thought about how everything could be different. But would not be. She hadn't transmissionally sighed though. She hadn't cast around for eyes. Even allowing for the antiquation which defines a woman alone in a bar as obviously offering something, she had continued to feel self-contained. And so it had remained, until she didn't want to anymore.

That's when he came to the bar. She turned her head. He saw her. They spoke. She bought him a drink. They talked. He was funny. This was something she liked. And she decided she wanted to. She then invited him up and he was willing to go. It was pleasant, more than pleasant. She had no cause for complaint and he also gave the impression of having enjoyed himself. If the earth didn't move, that was never expected. It was not even desired.

It was afterwards that the damage began to be done, when they covered the smoke detector and lit cigarettes up – his brand, and only one each. That was vaguely pioneering. She had never done that before and will admit to relishing such teenage carry-on, for all the five minutes it took. In any case the alarm hadn't gone off so, ostensibly, it was a foolish antic which had left no harm done – except perhaps for later on, somewhere on the bill. Anyway, they'd then decided on a mini-bar drink. Then on another and another cigarette and then done it all again. Yes, she thinks that was it, the moment of true catastrophe. The trouble was he was so easy to be with and she couldn't remember when she had last laughed this much in bed. That had, she will somewhat grudgingly admit, made the earth – just a little – shift. But, once that round was up too, she supposes the combined effects of jetlag and alcohol knocked them both into sleep. If they had been in his room she would probably have left. But his staying in hers, under the circumstance, hadn't felt particularly problematic – at least not in any way she had foreseen then.

The trouble dug in in the middle of the night when she awoke to find him still beside, eyes wide, and looking directly at her. 'What?' she thinks she may have muttered. 'Can't you guess?' he had said and, from the way he'd smiled, naturally enough, she could. 'Just let me do this then,' she had replied and, reaching up somewhere above their heads, turned the air conditioning off.

Yes, in an evening of unusual slips, turning the air conditioning off was probably significant. She thinks she could, if she wished, lay her guilt squarely at the foot of humidity paralysis – if guilt is what she's obliged to feel. It certainly caused the loose, warm muscles. The salt on their skin. It surely heightened the taint of the whiskey, or three, on their lips. Not that she was drunk, or even close. She's relieved drink wasn't the reason though. That's a method of blunder she called time on years ago – once it had begun to make the mornings-after hard because harder wasn't meant to be the point. Yet however useful this act of analysis is, can it provide a plausible theory for why, even whilst jammed in by this damned door, her body's isolation still feels intruded upon by the memory of his all over it?

No.

It does not.

You're going to have to do better than that.

Go beyond the body right to the mind because, she suspects, her pincer-like precision is about to become everything. It's not simply that he was handsomer, funnier, better than most in bed. He did not remind her of the past – that strand too has been excised. He asked no more than any other man ever had and seemed every bit as satisfied with what he had received. In fact, if she remembers correctly, initially anyway, it was she who'd wanted more . . . Not that it's of any consequence here. Now that the rogue element – the air conditioning – has likely been defined, she moves on to the idea of the closed door and its rightness. She won't be backing down on that opinion any time soon. Although the question could be asked: backing down on that opinion to whom? No one is asking. No one cares and it's not as if she really does either.

Which is not strictly true.

But.

She realises her critique of the experience is incomplete.

There was the other aberration too.

Yes.

In the morning they had, again. Her reservations allayed by his repetition of 'Yeah, I should get going too,' and 'Yeah, I really have to get going now.' But, ultimately, his not going at all and her not making him go. After that, seemingly having accepted he was going to be late, he had casually suggested they both get dressed and go out to get breakfast because 'This hotel's food is notoriously muck.' 'Somewhere in the city,' he'd suggested – apparently, he's been here a lot and therefore knows it quite well. She hadn't argued at this stage but also hadn't agreed. Did she favour it European-style though? Or could she handle it spicy? If so, he knew the perfect place. She'd like it. For him it tasted just like home. They could stroll across the river. No more than five minutes' walk . . . maybe ten. Then, in the apparent absence of all reason, she'd heard herself say, 'Yes,' and that, in fact, she was well able for this alleged spiciness. As her words fell into the air she could scarcely believe it. He, however, had. He said he'd just need to fetch his coat from downstairs but, given both that she was Irish and the projected temperatures, he'd guess she probably wouldn't need hers. Mercifully, if tardily, this brought her round. What the hell did he know about her and how dare he assume how she'd react to the weather and as for the taste of his homeland, well, why would she ever care about that? So, she assumed the position and cleared her throat. 'Actually,' she said. 'On second thoughts, I won't but thank you very much. Thank you for everything. It's been lovely . . . a lot of fun but I've got to get on so . . . if you wouldn't mind?'

His eyes when she'd said that. To understate, he wasn't pleased. 'Why not?' he'd asked. 'I'm the one late for a meeting and besides, you have to eat.' 'I just . . .' she'd said, then ummed and ahhed and then remembered she didn't owe him more than that and just said she'd rather not. If he displayed disappointment, she didn't notice it, now solely preoccupied by the possibility of it spreading across her own face. To expedite her discomfort she'd expressed a wish that there would be no hard feelings. A good time had been had but more didn't make sense as they were both only briefly in Texas and didn't know when they would be again. He had heard her out, even nodded his head, and yet seemed to remain unconvinced. The unforeseen consequence of this, although he'd complied and swiftly dressed, was that she herself had begun to be less certain of the grounds for her stance. The thing about the coat, he'd obviously meant as a joke. And she actually was kind of interested in the taste of his home. Plus, after last night, he no longer felt totally unknown and perhaps he felt that too. These thoughts, in their turn, must have been what caused her to behave in a fashion which she now considers, frankly, ridiculous. Specifically, when he'd said, 'Well, I'd better get on then,' she had crossed the whole room to kiss him goodbye. And with a greater enthusiasm than her dismissal justified. Then she opened the door. He went out. She closed it behind him and has stood there ever since willing him, if she's honest, to come back again. He appeared to have gone though, she heard the lift. The corridor had been empty when she first looked out. But then he had. Rung and knocked. Like a fool she'd opened up but, just as suddenly, remembered to not and quickly slammed it on him again. She knows her own mind, if nothing else, after all this time but . . . No, no ands and buts. She does know her own mind and this is not it. She is decided already and must not allow that choice to ever become undone. So, what will happen next? she wonders. Nothing will happen next. You have decided that nothing can.

She attempts to take comfort in the knowledge of her impeccable reasoning. After all, her record in these matters is clean. The years of residua circumvented should not be superseded flippantly. She is certain of the rightness of all of this. So, she ushers herself back towards the listlessness that has, for all these years, kept her in the manner which she wishes she preferred. Collected. Other side of the glass. But she liked his face. She liked his laugh and the weird way their bodies kept insisting on contact. This, however, does not alter the fact that the only place for impulse is in her past. She knows this. She has made it like that so everything occurring, after the old life stopped, would simply be an again. A kind of repeat. Nothing new. Pathetic really, when she thinks of it. If she allowed herself to, she might admit she's grown tired of her own loneliness, which she really doesn't want to have yet. Because it has come to be all I know.

   *so*

   *so*

   *so*

### The Imagined Room

A man told me a story, and it wasn't just a story, and he thought it would make me run. And if that ending to his story had proved to be the story? Some choices are made only once, but that other path still reconsiders its merit within me now and then. My eye pressed to a spyhole in an unfamiliar hotel appears to be one such occasion.

So.

She sees myself standing in an imagined hotel room all arrayed like a Victorian bedchamber I've repurposed from some film. Four-poster bed and bolster. Only bare bulb lit – an invented authenticity but . . . I am inventing this so I can deck it out in any way I want. Conversely now, a real truth: it would have been my first hotel. If not the Savoy of my imaginings, he would have taken care to make it decent. He'd have been conscientious about that because I was so young, showing up there in the middle of the night and then . . . would have been staying on my own. I think he would have walked me to the foyer. He would have seen me in and ensured all the details were in order – breakfast ordered, payment taken – before taking his final leave of me at the lift doors or foot of the stairs. Would he have leant in to kiss my cheek goodbye? I can't imagine him having not but, if coming here was the choice I'd opted for, we would already have been different. And, hard as it may be to gauge how we'd have introduced that space, this decisive going of our separate ways would certainly suggest a start. That said, now I'm in bed with the purely speculative any possibility might become fact.

Therefore, continue on.

Goodnight.

And to you.

Guilt and I step into the lift alone. While I press the button, guilt notices how quickly he turns and is glad when the doors slide shut. Then, aerial inside with the desolation I've wrought, I offer only silence to the joltering through floors. I have never been here, in either respect. Air freshener impeding the reek of my own stale smoke. But in the scuffed parquet, and polished rail, I detect traces of what may have been a heyday. Admittedly this is probably because I have no idea what to expect. There are no bell-boys in red suits or anything like that, which might have been a disappointment in another life – the one where my first hotel is an extravagant gift in some far-off shared future which now will not be reached. I don't want to think about that and force myself inside every second so none of me is anywhere else. I am here, only here. I grip my room key. It's too soon for the plastic cards – not that I'd have known to miss them. Besides which, all of this is theoretical and I have nothing to prove . . . not least regarding my lack of expertise about hotel room security, thirty-five years ago.

God.

I feel the lift stop. I see the doors part. There are plaques with arrows. I take a left. The dank art hanging in no way distracts for who cares about hay and wains? Instead I aim for the broad brass 36, nailed about Christ-height on a white gloss crucifix. I go to it. I try the key. I turn it. I open it. I enter in. I close it shut behind my back. And suddenly I am all by myself, standing somewhere new.

So.

Now I am in that hotel room. Brown furniture. Brown drapes. A quick, and heedlessly, packed bag dangling by my leg. I slide the chain. I turn the lock. I probably, definitely, take my coat off and hang it on the door. Then I see myself, in her youth and shock, walk across the room – certain that she is indeed crossing it, uncertain of all else she is doing. Beneath her though, the very carpet conspires with the faux Victorian theme: cubes and blocks in beige and brown, gold and fawn-tipped leaves. Autumnal, would've crossed my mind, despite the mid-June heat, as if I had already passed through time and found myself in August. Oh, to be safe in August, far beyond this insoluble here – I might have thought. I would have thought. I think I would . . . maybe. But the air itself would have held me there, close to the knowledge it could only be summer. Even in the flat of night the mineral fumes London respires would have given it away. Also, I doubt there'd have been air conditioning there then but, if there was, I'd have been baffled by the mechanism. Dials and buttons I don't recognise are best left alone I'd have thought and for God's sake don't break anything. Then I would have wished for him. Then I close the sides of the present down. I hold myself still in this alien place in which I have chosen to be. Having plumped for this unknown over something and, more importantly, over someone why is not too much to ask. But I'm not yet prepared for that. I'll have to gather myself closer into sync.

So, I notice the solitary window is slightly ajar. Single-glazed. Held unsteadily by an old rope sash. Through it I see the matching windows of the hotel opposite. Then – because I now usually do so, chances are, I would have then too – I go across the room with the intention of sliding it up. And do. And pull the nets out of the way. Above me, a moon and cloudless sky. There might be stars beyond the night flights but the glow makes it tricky to tell. Inevitably, my – as yet utterly untravelled self covets the journeys those aeroplanes make. The cities their dozing passengers will see – Byzantium springs to mind, irrationally, but I am a romantic back then. More reasonably, the oceans they'll sail across in their sleep. What continents will be waiting once they awake and bother to open their travel-bored eyes – I never seem to imagine specific travellers but then I haven't met any of them yet. What I don't fantasise is that they too head to hotels. Only skyscrapers. Yellow taxis. New York invariably, like that is the very best of the world, which would not have been an entirely incorrect assumption. I can think of worse places to rent a room and I've stayed

129

in quite a few of them since. But even with all of that said, I would not have been completely unaware of my having, in my own way, already come very far. And I probably would have accepted how that very far – so far from the innocence of where I started – had, until now, proved to be everywhere.

Or would I?

No. That won't fit. That's what I believed before imagining this situation I'm in. But tonight I am in a strange hotel and, therefore, an ulterior me. Yes, that surely must make sense. Unless, of course, in reality it doesn't. After all, it may be the case that the act of leaving him would not have left me changed. Perhaps, by my choosing to imagine coming to this place, I am merely absenting myself from what I don't know how to hear?

But I did know how to hear.

But that's not what you're referring to here.

I think I might be complicating this unhelpfully.

You are and you know you'll eventually get to that part of it anyway.

True.

Just keep going for now. Pick up from where you were.

So . . .

Maybe stars. Definitely flights. Heat and pushing the

window higher. Plane trees visible everywhere, becoming the scourge of my hay fever which – still being London green – I have yet to acquire.

Then I turn my eyes from the sky to the roofs, to the street. To the double-decker through whose top deck I can perfectly see. As expected, across is another hotel. Its white block facade almost identical but with not a single light on upstairs. Only a lamp above their entrance and, as I watch, even that goes out. Followed swiftly by the lamp shining up from below me. It is very early. Or very late? Dark before dawn, is that the hotel way? I have no yardstick by which to assess the hospitality industry's norms. Instead I consider all the lives asleep which those identically drawn brown curtains conceal – their also brown linings pressing against the indistinguishable nets. Some of their windows sit open too and, again, only an inch or so. What's occurring in the wonderlands of their symmetrised sleep? They must already be long hours in. Were they combing hair or brushing teeth, masturbating, reading, watching TV while I was awake, listening to him, having life peeled of its skin?

I don't know.

I don't know.

At that age I still thought I could hear anything. And I'd already heard plenty of things. But they'd only ever formed the backdrop before which I'd been trying to construct 'things' of my own. Tonight, this night, his life had taken the floor while I'd assumed the role of the sheet-clad chorus. I became the door through which his story passed into the realms of Can Never Be Unsaid. And it was hard to hear. Not that he was, or ever could have been, merely another sad voice confessing its baleful history – and that's not the vainglory of hindsight speaking, I knew it even then. He was more of a switchboard with the wiring ripped out whose adult life had been spent trying to intuit where it all plugged back in. And I had listened to him. And some of the details were very gruesome. And I was very young. And I still thought the house that the past lived in had a padlock on the door. That open didn't mean open eternally after. And even this imagined self comes too soon to be able to understand. I don't doubt though she's doing the very best she can. I should really get back to her.

So.

Given everything that he had said, it does seem unrealistic to pretend those hotel rooms across the way would've piqued much interest in me. I would have been, as I actually was, incorporating his story into what I had known. Full of those words and aspects of him which I could now suddenly see. The other hotel's clients' rest, or rest-inducing activities, would have never crossed my mind. In truth, I imagine I'd have stood like rootless in there, growing gnarled by this reveal of a history I found unbearable, and trying to make some shape of it I could more easily name. Trying to make some shape of it that would justify my running away. Then finding, inevitably, the ache which comes after pain hurts far longer and more than the blow. Shame might be the name for it – it usually is – for the discovery of being less than the person you offered to be. I don't doubt I'd have been feeling it and it would not have been entirely undeserved.

But no, back to this – the exercise will be futile if these digressions persist. So, I stand looking out at the hotel opposite. Then, with the Greek chorus returned to its place, and me reassuming an imagined centre stage, I decide – once another night bus passes by – I . . . I will look down onto the road.

I choose what I want to see. I know I am imagining this. I, in the here and now, am wilfully abstracting my own history. Because? There are a number of answers to this but today's will be: I can never find my past where I think I've left it and, in his designated role as catalyst, he is the worst offender of all. He will never just lie down where he lay. I keep discovering him wandering around inside me again. And the worst of it is, he will never allow me not to be the girl he knew back then. But, while I know what he means and he has the best of intentions, she can be very hard to endure. She was always so sure. I suppose we both admired, and now regret, her loss of certainty.

Oh . . .

Dear God, save me from this.

And he can't, because he doesn't exist.

Instead I cast a flustered eye down.

Down to there.

And I see him below in the empty street, lowering his head to light his cigarette. If that's the case, he'll be using a match because he's left his lighter at home. I think I'll remember noticing it lying by his bed as we left. Unusual for him not to remember it himself but unusual is how I'd describe this whole night. So, while I tentatively signed the hotel registration slip, I imagine him asking the sleepy desk clerk for a matchbook. Then, he'd have quickly pocketed it before we said goodbye. I'm glad to see him lighting up. He should have something to take the edge off and it could be so much worse. I can't say that I'd say no to one either, and this is a smoking room, but I've also forgotten mine – probably at his too. This is the kind of little punishment I enjoy giving myself for being unable for what he shared. Because he wouldn't have punished me. He'd have been so keen to prove he wasn't holding it against me that he wouldn't have noticed an extraneous thing – which would surely include a lighter folded into a duvet on the unmade bed in his room. Unlike me who, having chosen to be up against nothing, now has plenty of free time to observe.

Which I do.

When the cigarette lights, he drops back his head. Inhale and exhale. I think he'll think he's done right, finding me this room. And he has too, but is he now suffering pangs over what else he decided to do? How well I've come to know that dread: the stomach come-uppance of disclosures made to someone who turned out to be entirely unsuitable for any such disclosures at all. That's not how I want him to think of me, and I'd rather he wouldn't regret anything but even then – even imagining – I knew him sufficiently well to hazard an accurate guess. Besides, from my vantage point up here, I can see the dejection in the angle of his shoulders. I would really rather not see but the grey streetlight he loiters beneath refuses to become my accomplice in this. He is the one with whom it forms an alliance, arrang-ing itself in such a fashion as to ensure I see his every twinge. In how he rubs his eyes. In how he rubs the back of his neck. I can see all of it. So, when he drops the match, I shut the sash. As he walks away, I pull the curtains tight. I will tolerate nothing being privy in here to the standard I have failed to meet out there. Either that or I can no longer bear looking at the empty place where he stood.

Too late, too late will be the cry and now, on top of this, here comes the time to be the choice you made.

So.

I stand golden in the sixty-watt of my brown room but, cloistered in here, what future do I imagine I've chosen? As I've just fled from serious complexity, one more greatly inclined to be infantilising, I would expect. But who imagines alternative personal futures fraught with difficulty? Why would I have? Or no, why would I have then? When you are young Better usually hovers around all the entrances or, at worst, The Same. Even back at brass tacks, when I remained in his room, it never occurred to me that what would become of us both was in the offing at all. Small mercies, I suppose, and that sort of thing. But perhaps – to lie about this differently – it all worked out another way? And why not? I hear you can try anything.

So.

When I entered the room, the curtains were already shut. I never looked out, or bestowed sleep, on the hotel residents across. Didn't notice a bus. Didn't look at the street. Didn't invent the J'accuse of an inanimate object.

Never watched him walk off down the road. This version has its own consistency. As mentioned before, by the act of leaving, I may already have been different. It's plausible at least. In which case, I may not have been as predictable as I think. But herein lies the rub of the antithetical thread: envisaging how other choices might have constructed the life you've actually lived. Years could atrophy in the ciphering of it and as I've no wish to embark on a mid-life crisis – although I think we can already take that as read – it would probably be to no avail anyway. We cannot know what we were not or what we were not to become. Besides, why should I permit myself this alternative view? Its companion in logic I have always refused: the claim of not recognising yourself in your past or of failing to possess any significant insight into the whys of what you did. Despite the mess, and so much mess, I've consistently forbidden myself those spurious comforts because . . .

I knew myself.

I always knew myself.

Which means that kind of declaration is as impossible to make as denying the inescapable state of knowing myself has invariably made matters worse.

Well now.

I do like all these lines of words but they don't seem to be helping much with keeping the distance anymore.

Maybe I should add more again?

Maybe I should ruthlessly edit?

Maybe I should stop fucking around with language? It's not improving matters at all.

Funny, how unbearable I'm finding all of this, considering I'm only imagining it. I'm only confirming by deliberation what I once avoided by instinct – a future rife with regret. Which is not, in the current circumstance, wholly un-useful to do. In fact, it's most likely very useful to do and I should carry on. But then I'm sure, somewhere within, the answers are already flashing red to my dishonest questions. Because I know my grammar-frantic logic is only that. I've never had the slightest interest in being a trier-on of hats and, really, I'm as prone to contrariness as I ever was. Just because I *can* analyse from any which way up, doesn't mean I should.

Certainly, it doesn't mean I'm obliged to.

And, of course, I could just stop.

I could remove my eye from the spyhole and cease concocting all of this. I could hop in the shower. I could order up breakfast. I could go back to bed for a couple of hours and leave last night where it, proverbially, lay. I could forget this room I've imagined for myself, in which I've chosen to think I am safe. All of those options might be better, easier anyway. Then again, with the angst already stirred up perhaps I should gallantly embrace my choice of 'no more options' and get to the bitter end? Yes, perhaps. Why not run the whole godforsaken business to earth and finally, finally be done? Too soon, too soon might be the cry but when have I ever listened to that?

Go on then. Run it down.

Besides, no outcome need be set in stone.

Well . . . that's not what you have just been saying.

But.

Just go on.

Pick it up from . . .

Pick it up from here:

He had still left. I was still that. I am still at the hotel – I assume – standing bewildered. This is still the version in which I don't cross the room or make a beeline for the window. In this version I go to the desk. I turn on a lamp and let it illuminate whatever it wants. Perhaps I investigate the stationery drawer and wonder about keeping the pens? But I wouldn't want to risk him incurring any additional expense. In all honesty, I can't imagine it, giving a damn about headed notepaper or monogrammed envelopes. Perhaps I switch on the TV instead? And while even that is hard to credit, as I'm discarding what really happened, then anything might have, isn't that how this works? And why can't I? Why shouldn't I? Who would have blamed me if I'd left? No one, not really, apart from myself. Even he offered to get me this room because he'd thought I, conceivably, might. After all, this was also the first time in his life that his devils had been lined up publicly and called aloud by name. Well, spoken of in a dimly lit room to a woman with whom he was also in love. But a woman he knew was possessed of a few devils of her own, albeit differently. That's how he thought of it, I'd say. She had devils alright but none, as yet, she'd been complicit in the making of so he couldn't know how I'd react. Of course, that was all less important to me – bent, as I was, on biting into everything. But then, I didn't know how the past worked, not until much later on. Still, I heard the words and in time learned to read the shape. In some ways, for him, I became the shape. After all, I stayed. How could I not? And I go from this room to the room where he sat. I remember his face in the final words of it, like we were both up on some high place and a millstone had been lashed to his leg. As I sit again on that reimagined bed, I have no idea who sits here.

So often since then memories have dog-eared themselves but that night, in isolation, remains incomparably itself. Even after all these years, it still shows spectacularly clear and hurts like splinters in skin. The quiet we went, studying it. Him staring at his hand. The twitch

on his cheek. 'That's horrible,' I'd said. 'I know,' he'd
agreed and gotten off the bed. Somewhere in that rented
house someone else had come in. We'd held onto ourselves listening to them go up the stairs, into their room.
Ah, that's where the idea of a TV comes from – we'd
heard them turn theirs on. I had envied them their distance from us. That was when he'd said, 'If you want to
leave, I'll sort you out a room.' And I'd imagined myself
in some clean white bed, falling asleep, safe from it. 'It'
as if he and his history weren't intrinsic, which, as it
happens, I think was sort-of true. Is that now the same
for me too? Extrication isn't what I'm pursuing though.
Not really, not anymore. What I remember next is how
I answered him. But to place myself in this imagined
room, I must say something different like 'Yes, I think
you should,' or 'If you don't mind, that might be for the
best.' I wouldn't have been cruel to him about it, not
ever, just cruel enough to go. And, as I said, he wouldn't
have been angry, not even taken aback. He'd probably
have nodded. Dressed. Gone to the door. Put on his coat.
Waited for me to get into my clothes. I doubt he'd have
said another word, except – perhaps – as I packed up,
'Don't worry about your other stuff. You can collect it
whenever you want.' And I'm certain he'd have carried
the bag for me – 1 would've been too mortified to insist
he didn't. That would've been an indignity, for both of

us, too far. Then he'd have locked up. We'd have gone down the stairs and walked to whichever hotel he had in mind. Or maybe already knew. Somewhere nearby because of the hour. But not somewhere awful, for reasons already described. What is the point of this exercise again? All of this is long past done. He was not a man from whom I wanted to run, nor was I the type of young woman who thought the world could only work in one way. The crux is, a faint heart was never it, never the difficulty I struggled with. Quite the opposite.

But.

All these years later, I'm still thinking about that night. In some ways I think I've never stopped circling it, niggling at what it meant. About him. About me. It is my brightest, my one unalterable memory. No matter what use I put it to, it never fails to bloom. So, if in every life there must be a touchstone, then this one is irrefutably mine.

Because.

That night I heard a story that might have made me run. I learned how the body I had loved and touched had lived another life. Pitilessly, physically. In its recountment, guiltily. Even, when younger, brokenly, in ways similar to mine. And the unforeseen repercussion of hearing it was finding myself in the dark and adrift from the very person I had been throwing caution to the winds with. Not that it had never been previously intimated. It was more the all-engulfing nature it took which provided the ferocious surprise. After all, I knew he was more than twice my age and, naïve as I was I wasn't *that* naïve, so . . . what else would he have been at? Nowadays, I assume it was that naïveté though which beguiled him into those tells – and by 'beguiled' I mean beguiled himself for, in spite of this morning's suggestion of plot, I was never a one for games. I didn't think of myself as anything like bait. I would have considered that poor, preoccupied, as I was, with telling the truth – a folly I still struggle to resist. No matter. To the matter. I think it's safe to assume it was the guilelessness which drew him a little open, then persuaded him to a little more. And I had no idea what was going on, until I knew everything. 'Well, what harm can she do?' he later said was what he'd think or 'Why worry? She'll meet a boy her own age soon and I'll be off the hook. Fun while it lasts, with no foreseeable risk, et cetera et cetera.' All fair weather, I suppose, until he fell the whole way in and knew he had to tell out everything. Then we both found ourselves, unpreparedly, pinned by the weight of what his words brought. That night, tonight – if I'm doing my imaginative homework – I saw/see the world anew. That adulthood could be no freer of what had already been. All the awful evidence plain in his anonymous rack-up of bodies. The self-proliferated lies. His long revulsion at the satisfaction so little money can buy, and should not buy, which he already knew but had already done. How he'd lived with it all, for a long time, and not much of it well. And I saw his loneliness. I believed in it – it was as clearly on display as a horsehair shirt. But still I had flinched from its embodiment, as he knew I would. As he didn't know I wouldn't, if he were telling me now. Well, not from some of it because I am no longer in a position to judge – not that my judging him was the point. Only he thought that should be my right. I never wanted to, or truly did. Nevertheless, it left us both wrecked in its wake, for a time at least. Catching us and hobbling us where we had not thought to look, as if we believed, once exposed to the air, there might be no afterwards. But everything is about afterwards, as I have come to know. After it back then, I remember sitting on his bed, willing myself not to be afraid because I understood that whatever he had done – and been – was just bindings around a person who was really someone and that real someone, in his turn, saw beyond the bindings around me. That we two, regardless of the injunctions of our histories, were about to try another way through.

So.

As far as reasons for all this painful recollecting go, there's that. However, less dramatically and concealed beneath, there probably lies a greater truth. It might even be the idea upon which I built myself from – almost – my adult life's first breath. It existed before he and I ever met – although, in fairness, he was to prove a reasonably defining test. And it was knowing that to leave, rather than stay, would betray the most fundamental bargain I'd made which, at its very simplest, read: you be London, and I will rise to that. It's the kind of deal only youth can strike, in all its ignorance and hope. I won't even attempt to argue its part. Instead I will merely observe that to have proved unequal to its offer of everything, every kind of life – including all that terrible love – would not only have resulted in youthful illusions lost, I think it would have made a wasteland of me.

And there it is.

And so there it is.


That was difficult. But I got here in the end.


So now.

So now, what?

So now, have you gathered your rosebuds?

You know what you have to do.

I do.

So now, I do.

I stand in the hotel room I've imagined, imagining him walking home. The window, the bare bulb, the carpet, the desk – what would have to be paid for and what I could take – all dimming into generalities of themselves. All losing their reality because they were not and could never have really been. This is the end of imagination. How soon until the cock crows thrice? And all at once so much rides upon not hearing that. Every part of me knowing it is already past time to cross back over this counterfeit room. Put down your fake treachery. Put your coat on. Pick up your bag and unlock the door. Go into the corridor. Call for the lift. Step in, with no thought for what it once was and, as it opens again downstairs, run for all you are worth through the deserted foyer out onto the empty street. Face the glowering lamp but, holding nothing against it, just go to where he last stood. Look then and see the sun hint at itself in the east. Its awkward beginnings dragging into relief the now bus-less roads, the dusty trees, the black paint flaking from wrought-iron railings and beyond, into the morning distance, where his lank figure still retreats. Then, without knowing if every part of me will withstand what's now coming, in dreadful tests of time, call until he turns.

And I do.

Then.

Turn too and return again from this most fitly resolved past that was never really an option – primarily for its never having been an actual question – to the life which, in fact, exists. The one that requires now going Live to an Austin hotel. The one where the sweat on my palm blurs the view from the spyhole. The one where I listen inside for sounds outside in the hall. The one, apparently, fashioned from my own will. And what does my will think of me now?

Probably that it's tired of this tone. Of relentlessly reshuffling the deck of pseudo-intellectual garble which, if I'm honest, serves the solitary purpose of keeping the world at the far end of a very long sentence. And that will no longer do. And that will no longer be? This is the day. The hour. The minute.

And so?

I am beholden to no past, that much is clear. I am the last one standing in so many memories. Will I decide there can be more again? Or will I procrastinate at this door until the end of my days? Or will I choose to remember that there are some things I already know how to do?

*Austin* x

*Pisa*

*Paris*

Funchal

Austin x

Belfast

Galway

Brighton

Bruges

Hay-on-Wye

Borris

Liverpool

Austin x

Bantry

Helston

Liskeard

Edinburgh

Gothenburg

Boston

Austin x

Dublin

Dún Laoghaire

San Francisco

Austin x

*Inis Oírr*

*Listowel*

*Besançon*

*Toronto*

*Brussels*

*Prague*

*Berlin*

*Dublin*

*Montreal*

*Dublin*

*Cork*

*Austin* x

*Dublin*

*Zagreb*

*Austin* x

*London* x

ACKNOWLEDGEMENTS

Thanks to my agent, Tracy Bohan, without whose prompting this book would not exist.

Thanks to my editors, Alex Bowler and Mitzi Angel, whose patient attention it was in need of.

Thanks to Fergal McBride, Marietta Smith, Phoebe Harkins and Ross Macfarlane, for their many kindnesses.

And thank you most of all to William and Éadaoin Galinsky, without whom my life would be very strange indeed.

## A Note About the Author

Eimear McBride is the author of the novels *The Lesser Bohemians* (winner of the James Tait Black Prize) and *A Girl Is a Half-formed Thing* (winner of the Women's Prize for Fiction, the Kerry Group Irish Novel of the Year Award, and the Goldsmiths Prize). She was the inaugural creative fellow at the Samuel Beckett Research Centre (University of Reading), and she occasionally writes for *The Guardian*, *The Times Literary Supplement*, the *New Statesman*, and *The Irish Times*.